Transformations

by Bernard Doove

TRANSFORMATIONS

A "Forest Tales" story.

Copyright © 1999 – 2008 by Bernard Doove

All rights reserved, including the right to reproduce this book, or any portions thereof, in any form.

A production of *The Chakat's Den* – www.chakatsden.com

Cover art by Stephanie Stone

Interior art: see back page for full list

All graphics/art in this book are copyrighted by their respective artists. Any reproduction of these materials in any format without the expressed, written consent of the copyright holders is prohibited. Any resemblance between the fictional characters and situations in this book and real-life persons or situations is coincidental.

Contents

Foreword 4

Introduction 5

Part One – P.O.V. : Forestwalker 7

Part Two – Learning About Oneself 54

Part Three – P.O.V. : Dale 112

Illustration Credits 162

FOREWORD

I never set out to be a writer. My first story came about solely because I wanted to show people what chakats were like as people rather than just the cold facts that I had published in my *Introduction To Chakats*, an article that also has grown considerably as a direct result of my stories. Having written one story though, I realised that I still had much to tell about my chakats family, so I wrote another. And another. And another. At the time that I am formatting this paperback version, I have completed the thirtieth in the *Forest Tales* series, and fast approaching the sixtieth story in the Chakat Universe. This quite amazes me, and I still have several more ideas to write up!

Ironically, with *Transformations*, I have come full circle, because it deals with a human learning what it is to be a chakat. I like transformation stories, and I have read ones that have ranged from excellent to horrendous. I was determined that mine would not be the latter! Hopefully, even people who have never read one of my other stories will quickly get a feel for them. Most of all, I hope that everyone will see chakats are just people too despite their different customs, and not just some kinky hermaphrodite species.

I would like to dedicate this book to several people...

First: Roy D. Pounds II, a very good friend and an extraordinary artist. He was one of the first people to bring the chakats to life with drawings, and his works in return have inspired my stories in me. He has selflessly done so much for me, and I am so pleased that his art graces these pages.
Second: Boyce Garald Kline Jr is more than a character in my stories. He's my real life friend, virtually a brother to me, and a source of encouragement and inspiration.
Third: Kacey Miyagami (née Maltzman), who genuinely seems to like my weird characters and ideas, and who almost always captures their likeness perfectly first try. She is a wonderfully talented artist, and I'm happy to call her my friend.
Fourth: All those artists and writers who have drawn or written about chakats because the characters excited them, and not merely because they were being paid for it. You people have helped make the Chakat Universe the wonderfully complex and exciting thing it is today.
Thank you to all of you.

Bernard Doove (a.k.a. Chakat Goldfur) goldfur@chakatsden.com

INTRODUCTION

The early 21st Century saw a quantum leap in genetic engineering, but while that was an immense boon to medical science, the less altruistic side to it was the money to be made from it. The most obvious change was the introduction of modified animals that were smarter, more useful, more... human. These were the first true anthropomorphs, and while many were used for a variety of tasks that allowed humans to spend less time labouring, there was more money to be made by supplying war beasts to the military, and sex toys to the increasingly decadent populace. Some countries abhorred the new morphs, as did many religions, eventually becoming a greater source of dissidence than almost anything else. Disagreements broke down into fights, and fights into wars. By the year 2050, the first major battle of what would become known as the *Gene Wars* began. These battles spread like wildfire through almost every country in the world, involving every human and morph without distinction.

Forty years would pass before a worldwide armistice would be declared. There were no winners. Whole nations had been wiped out, much fertile ground had been rendered unusable for centuries, and the human race was reduced to a pitiful fraction of its formerly immense population. But many morphs had also survived, outnumbering the remaining humans in total, if not by individual species. To rebuild civilisation, humans needed the morphs badly, and they raised them to the level of humans, undoing the modifications that had kept them enslaved. Morphs were given equality with humans, and with that incentive, willingly worked alongside their former masters in what would be called the Great Reconstruction. Utilising the special abilities of various morphs highlighted their usefulness, and new genetic laboratories worked at creating new species to fill those needs that the diminished population could no longer deal with.

Some of the more intriguing creations were the taurforms – possessing the four-legged feral body of wolves, foxes, or felines, but possessing an upright humanoid torso where the neck would normally be. In principle, they resembled the legendary centaurs, only they were fully furred and with faces befitting their base species. Of these, one of the latest created was the *chakat*. Unlike those before them, they were created with additional goals in mind, something representing much of the best of what humanity had to offer. Additionally, they were true hermaphrodites. Some people loathed them, but most came to love them. However, not even the most ardent wanted to *become* one!

"... MY TWIN SISTERS?"

PART ONE
P.O.V. : Forestwalker

I stood in the doorway, momentarily stunned by the sight of my sister, Goldfur... *both* of hir! Two chakats, centauroid felines patterned like a cougar, faced me, identical in every detail of fur pattern. The same golden-brown fur and waist-long golden-blonde hair tied in a ponytail; absolutely identical dark markings on the muzzle; same lengthy prehensile tail. They even smelled exactly the same. The only difference that I could make out was that they wore different duty uniforms, which was no help as they were both types that Goldfur wore on different occasions. One looked agitated and depressed, while the other had an air of curiosity and anticipation. A Star Corps officer, a wolf morph named Commander Redfang, looked at me expectantly while I tried to puzzle this out.

I had come here to pick up Goldfur from the spaceport. Hir foxtaur lifemate, Garrek, was away at his home village and I had volunteered to drive hir back and forth. Shi was currently working on the Corps' geosynchronous space station and was beaming there and back from the transporter facilities at the spaceport. Shi had taken on the long overdue work of major maintenance and upgrades to the station because it kept hir close to home for the duration. It was only a short time after the birth of hir and Garrek's second child whom they'd just named Tailstalker because of hir penchant for chasing everybody's tails. Rather than go on another deep space assignment so soon, Goldfur had elected to take this job so that hir cub could be left in the family's care in hir absence. Star Corps' maintenance department was ecstatic because they seldom got the services of such highly rated technicians as Goldfur because they were all needed for the starship missions. Garrek normally would be working with hir as usual, but was taking care of foxtaur clan duties for a few days.

On the other hand, I was mere days away from delivering the cub sired by the Admiral and I had just gone on maternity leave, which left me with little to do. I suppose Goldfur could have made hir own way back and forth, but we both enjoyed being able to spend some time together, just we two sisters.

This had been just another normal trip to the spaceport to pick up Goldfur and I had been waiting in the Corp's large foyer for my sister to arrive. I had arrived a little bit late and was mildly surprised that Goldfur wasn't there already. I wasn't too concerned though because delays weren't too unusual, but I was surprised again though to hear my name paged over the public address system:

"Paging Chakat Forestwalker. Would Shir Forestwalker please report to the information desk for an important message."

I walked over to the information desk where the young lass behind it smiled in recognition and passed a note to me. I grinned back and thanked her. Jenny was an acquaintance whom I'd made long ago, although we'd rarely had the opportunity to chat much. I looked at the message and saw that it was from Goldfur. It said: "Forest. I have been detained by a major problem and it might be some time before I will be able to meet you. Sorry for the delay. If you want to go back home and await my call, let me know. Otherwise, I'll be out as soon as possible. Love, Goldie."

I sighed. "Oh well, these things happen, I suppose," I thought to myself. I ended up talking a lot with Jenny, spending more time with her than in several months. However, she couldn't talk too much because she was on duty, so I wandered around the lobby, examining everything in detail. The Star Corps building wasn't the only facility at the spaceport, but it featured one of the most impressive lobbies. Its vaulted ceiling had been painted a matt black that soaked up all reflected light. However, this didn't mean that it was a dark and gloomy room. Far from it! For the space between floor and ceiling was filled with one of the largest and most elaborate holograms that I had ever seen. The entire solar system was represented there. Each planet could be seen in magnificent detail, and their associated moons were all in their orbits. Comets and asteroids wove through the astral plane, and the hologram sun was the main source of light for the room. Places like the information desk were islands shaped and placed in such a way as to suggest that they were objects like starships or space stations. A few more holograms ringed the room, each showcasing one of the Corps' projects: Terraformed worlds, new colonies, even the discovery of the extinct Arborian culture with which I had been involved were proudly displayed. It was magnificent and fascinating, but after a couple of hours of looking at it, I had had more than my fill of it.

At last, the word came through for me to go meet up with Goldfur. I was directed to go to the office of the duty officer and, after asking for directions, I headed there promptly. The rest of the building, although not unpleasing in its decor, was much more functional and easy to navigate. I knocked on the door and a voice said, "Enter!", so I did. There, the first thing that I saw was a wolf morph seated behind the desk, a name stand on it telling me his name was Commander Kylan Redfang. It was an unspectacular office, neatly but sparsely decorated and, seeing as it was shared by various duty officers, lacking a lot of personal touches that everyone adorns their territory with. It was also a very large room, which is why I didn't immediately notice the other occupants. The wolf morph wordlessly drew my attention with his eyes to the corner of the room to my right. I turned, only to be confronted by the sight of identical twin sisters. Nobody said anything, evidently waiting from a response from me. I was confused. Obviously they both couldn't be my sister, yet they were completely alike in all respects... wait! There was *one* difference. I turned to the one on the right and said, "Okay! Would you care to explain the meaning of your doppelganger here?" I jerked my thumb in the direction of the other.

The Star Corps officer shook his head in amazement, while Goldfur's muzzle split in a grin as shi stepped up to hug me in proper greeting. "It's a long story, Forest, but basically, shi used to be a human male named Dale Perkins, believe it or not. Shi was cloned into a facsimile of my body because of a transporter

accident." Goldfur's expression became serious. "Shi came within a hair of being killed. This was the result."

Dale's expression had barely changed. Shi...? He...? Oh, the hell with it! I'd stick with 'shi' as that was hir current form. Shi spoke up then, hir words slurred and barely understandable. "Prraps ib woodb beem bedda if ah *had* died." Hir voice sounded hollow and with a hint of utter hopelessness. I was shocked to hear such words come out of a chakat's mouth because a zest for life was one of our characteristics. Of course, shi was a chakat in body only.

"I don't want to hear any more of that sort of talk, Ensign!" Commander Redfang said severely. "We'll be investigating every possible means of reversing this. It's only a matter of time." Dale nodded, unconvinced. The wolf then turned to me. "As for you, Shir Forestwalker, are you going to tell me how you could tell who was who, or are you going to make me die of curiosity? I couldn't tell even the slightest difference in looks, voice or scent."

"Simple," I replied. "One of the lesser known abilities of chakats is our mild empathic talent. This ability lets us form special bonds with our loved ones. I could sense emotions coming from both, but only my sister possessed that unique link once I looked for it."

"Told you shi'd pick me!" Goldfur said smugly.

"Alright! Alright! You win already!" The wolf threw up his hands in mock surrender.

"So, what happens now?" I asked.

"We were just debating that when you arrived," Goldfur replied. "The Commander here thinks Dale should stay at the base while they poke and pry hir. I say that all that will prove is that shi has the body of a chakat! I feel that shi should come with us and we can show hir how to cope with hir new form while the technicians investigate how this happened and how shi might be

restored to human form."

The wolf looked ready to argue further, then sighed and shrugged. "There's no precedent for this. I suppose we can always call in Ensign Perkins if we really need him... hir... oh, whatever."

I looked at my sister. "Are you sure you want to do this, Goldie? We don't exactly have experience with this either."

"I think we should, Forest. Besides, if it wasn't for me, shi wouldn't be in this predicament and I feel kind of responsible."

"Of course, Ensign Perkins would be completely dead if you hadn't acted," the wolf added, "So I don't want you beating yourself up about it either, you hear?"

Goldfur grinned. "Don't worry about that. I don't regret my actions, but I do take responsibility for them. You don't mind if Dale uses the guest room, sis?" shi asked me.

"Shouldn't be a problem," I agreed. With Garrek absent, Goldfur was sleeping with the rest of us anyway, freeing up the room. "What about you, Dale? Are you okay with this?"

Dale shrugged. "Muh life seems to be in roons, no madda what I chooos," shi replied in my sister's voice. It was eerie, but also disturbing because of the hopelessness in hir tone.

"Okay, if that's settled, I've got other problems to deal with. I know how to get in touch with you if needed, so get going!" With that, the Commander shooed us out of the office.

At that point, I got to see something that would have clued me sooner as to which sister was the real one. Up until then, Dale had been sitting on the floor in front of the desk, fidgeting slightly, hir tail twitching occasionally. Goldfur got up and urged hir double to do the same. Now, as shi walked to the door, it was a clumsy and awkward movement. Hir tail dragged on the floor and shi seemed ready to trip over hir own paws at any moment. Of

course! Shi'd never learned to walk on four feet and shi must be fighting hir body's instincts constantly. It seemed that the first things that we needed to teach hir were the very basics! Goldfur stayed at hir side in case shi faltered and I took up the other side. We supported hir as shi occasionally stumbled, but we were both startled as shi gave a sudden yelp as we exited the building. It turned out that the automatic doors had closed on hir tail lagging so far behind the rest. Shi hadn't really been hurt, but had been given an unexpected scare. To ensure that it wouldn't happen again, I picked up the end of hir tail, swung it around hir body and handed it to hir, saying, "Here! Until you learn to control your tail, you'd be better off holding onto it!"

Shi took it gingerly, as if it was a delicate, fragile thing. "Muh tail..." Dale said with a touch of wonder in heir voice. Shi seemed fascinated by the thought of actually having one. I patted hirs with mine, with a renewed appreciation for our sensitive, expressive appendage. "I think you'll learn to like it," I said.

"Umm, thangs... thankks," Dale said without taking hir eyes of the furry limb in hir hands.

We continued on to my vehicle, Dale hugging hir tail to hirself. While hir mind was focused on that though, shi stopped thinking so much about actually walking, and therefore stopped fighting hir new body's instinctive gait. We got to the PTV without further incident and only had minor difficulty getting hir onboard. It was a little like assisting a very elderly Longtail and had a touch of familiarity about it. Dale seemed fascinated by the taur-adapted vehicle. These Personal Transport Vehicles had only a single large door on either side, as well as a hatchback. These allowed us to easily step inside and settle ourselves on the moulded couches in front and beside the doors. Swing-away backrests made the journey more comfortable and safer because of the built-in harnesses. The couches in front of the hatchback door were smaller, adapted for carrying our cubs. Last but not least, it was a CS model, standing for Chakat Special, meaning that it was fitted with controls that enabled me to drive the vehicle with just my handpaws if necessary, leaving my true hands free to do other

things. It was a beautiful, sleek machine, and I was very proud of it. It was just a pity that a vehicle that was big enough for several taurs ended up being so big that it was hard to park!

As we left the parking lot and headed for the freeway, I turned to Goldfur and said, "Okay, now that we have some time, I'd like some explanations."

"Explanations?" echoed Goldfur.

"Details! Telling me that this was a transporter accident was a glib statement that told me almost nothing. What really happened? Tell me how we ended up with a cloned 'sister'. I want every little fact!"

"Alright, you asked for it." Shi took a deep breath and started hir tale. "The shift on the space station had ended and, after packing up my tools, I headed for the transporter room. It had been a pretty typical day of repairing broken-down equipment and installing upgrades wherever needed. It would be going a lot quicker if Garrek was here to help me," shi said wistfully. I nudged hir to get hir mind back on the subject. "Anyway, this day I had been doing an EVA to try to find a fault in one of the communication arrays. Turned out to be a micrometeorite puncture causing an intermittent failure. I replaced the defective unit, and as I was stowing it in a suit compartment, I noticed a starship rendezvousing with the station. I recognised it as one of the Corps' science vessels, the *Archimedes*. It had just returned from an extended mission and I took the time to watch it docking. It was something that I rarely got to see from that vantage point. However, I knew that its arrival meant an influx of personnel onto the station. Sure enough, when I got to the transporter station, there was a queue of people waiting for their turn to beam down. As I joined the line, Dale arrived with a trolley-load of goods. I was rather curious about all the stuff that he'd brought with him, so I struck up a conversation.

Goldfur paused and lowered hir voice to a murmur that was intended only for my ears. "Truthfully, I also found him quite handsome. Tall and rugged... mmrrrr!" I grinned in response, but I also noticed Dale's ears twitch. I wonder if shi'd heard what my sister had said. After all, shi now had hir same acute hearing now. I mentally shrugged, unable to do anything about it either way, and turned my attention back to Goldfur.

"Anyway," shi continued in a normal tone, "We got to talking about his voyage, and he was eager to show off some of the exotic goods that he had picked up. He'd been one of the last to get into line to be beamed down to Earth because he'd brought samples of exotic foods from various worlds, plus many other alien artefacts such as an ornate wooden carving and a statuette carved of some ivory-like substance, all of which needed to go through quarantine to be thoroughly tested or decontaminated before transportation down to the planet. So far Earth hasn't acquired some alien plague and the Corps is doing its best to see that none ever will. I'd been especially interested in the ivory because of Admiral Kline's enjoyment of such relics."

"Thuh Mordoks call id a *kasmek*," Dale spoke up, momentarily distracted from hir plight. "Id was a statchoo of their good-lugg... luck... spirrid. Fad lodda good id did me!"

"A kasmek, that's right. I'd forgotten that in the recent events." Goldfur nodded to Dale then continued. "He'd brought back an extraordinary amount of goods, something that would prove to be an important factor in his survival. Our wait passed quickly this way and soon it was my turn to beam down, which went quite normally. I paused to say hello to the transporter technician, Angela Frost, an old friend of mine. When the signal came for the next beam-down, everything started normally. The containment field was sparkling as the incoming plasma filled it when suddenly alarms started going off. Angela frantically started trying to deal with it, attempting to complete the transport, but finding she still lacked Dale's pattern. Finally she slapped him into a holding pattern. She urgently asked me to watch over the controls while she tried to find out what had happened. She knew that I had the necessary qualifications for the job, especially since I had maintained and fine-tuned many of them. Believe me, a transporter is something in which you don't want even the slightest glitch. She contacted the station and we were both concerned to hear a babble of confused and highly agitated voices at the other end. Finally we were able to determine that there had been an accident of some kind. As reports came in, we were getting more and more concerned. Matter transportation is an extremely energy intensive operation, which is why bulk cargoes still get space-lifted by shuttles or the unique Quange Cosmoliners. We could not maintain the continuous energy drain of the holding pattern for long. On top of this, there's no such thing as a perfectly lossless transport, but usually the process causes no harm whatsoever. However, it is cumulative and as the seconds passed, we got more and more worried about Dale's condition. First we thought that there had been some sort of power loss, but all transporters have their own emergency power supplies. Then the word came through that there had been an explosion that had damaged the pattern buffer. Now the buffer is just a gigantic memory bank; there's nothing in there that *can* explode, and it has more surge protectors than any other system aboard the station. That meant that the explosion had been deliberate, something that sent a shudder through us both. The station's transporter officer finally confirmed our worst fears: "Catastrophic failure with total pattern loss," he confirmed. "I'm so very sorry."

"Wait a minute!" I interjected. "If you lost Dale's pattern, how can shi be here now, albeit in a new body?"

"How much do you know about how a transporter works?" Goldfur asked.

"Not a lot, I suppose. Generally, the transporter scans you, converts you into energy, transmits you to your destination, then converts you back into matter."

"Not even close, I'm afraid," Goldfur said with a shake of hir head. "For starters, if you converted all that mass into energy, you'd have the equivalent of a nuclear bomb go off. There's no way of containing that much energy, or even a fraction of it actually. $E=mc^2$, remember?"

"I know. I *did* do physics at school," I replied with a little sarcasm. "I was just describing it in popular terms."

"Sorry, but that description is way off the mark, and in order to understand properly what happened today, you need to know a more accurate one. There's a lot of technobabble though."

"Go on, we've got plenty of time," I urged, not intending to let hir off easily.

Goldfur leaned back in hir seat, composing hir thoughts. I stole a glance at Dale who looked completely disinterested. I sighed. I had hoped to get hir involved in the conversation, telling hir part, trying to keep hir mind off the situation. Obviously that wasn't working, but at least I was learning something new. Goldfur commenced hir explanation. "I'll try to keep this as non-technical as possible. Nudge me if I start getting too involved."

I nodded and shi continued. "Firstly, matter transportation was made possible by the discovery of a means of exciting matter into a quasi-energetic state. Commonly called plasma, this material possesses properties found in both matter and energy. It has the essential cohesiveness of matter, so it doesn't simply explode, but it can also be heterodyned onto a carrier signal and transmitted through the ether to a receiver in the manner of an energy beam. However, the plasma cannot exist under normal conditions, so the establishment of a containment field is the first step. It is this that you see sparkling during the transport process, not something being converted into energy. The next step is to set up a stasis within the containment field. In order to scan an object to create its pattern, that object needs to be as motionless as possible, and that right down to the molecular level. To do this, time virtually needs to be brought to a nearly complete halt."

"Good heavens! This *is* a lot more complex than I had thought," I exclaimed.

Goldfur nodded. "It gets worse. The transporter is by far the most complex device on a ship or space station, and possibly anywhere else. Anyway, when the stasis is established, the object is scanned down to the molecular level, with the position of each being mapped for the creation of the pattern."

"I thought you'd have to map it to the atomic level?" I queried.

"Thankfully, no. The cohesiveness of the plasma actually *remembers* the position of individual atoms, otherwise it would be an even more difficult process than it already is. Once the pattern is complete, there is another critical step before changing the physical state of a person."

"Another? I always thought that was all there was to it?"

"If you'll stop interrupting me, I'll explain!" my sister said with some asperity.

"Sorry. Please go on." I said contritely. I thought I heard a muffled snort from our passenger, so my questioning was perhaps having a side benefit.

"The true secret of the success of the transporter is called the mind-matrix. When the transporter was first created, it seemed like a perfect success. A chakat named Summerbreeze first worked out the means of converting, transmitting and reconverting matter for transportation purposes. All the test objects that shi had sent through the mechanism had checked out perfectly. Both mechanical and electronic gadgets worked absolutely normally after being sent through. Plants were the next things to be tried out, and they all grew healthily after going through the process. Careful analysis could find nothing wrong with them. It was time to try it out on a test animal, and that was when tragedy struck. A foolishly overconfident and eager assistant, instead of using a lab rat, put himself onto the transporter platform, wanting to be the first person to be beamed somewhere. Shi came through perfectly healthy, but a drooling idiot. Hir brain was completely wiped of all the higher thinking processes. Only the automatic functions such as maintaining breathing, etcetera, remained. Summerbreeze was devastated because that assistant was also hir niece, Joyleap. Shi ordered that nobody was to try transporting themselves without hir strict permission. Testing on various animals proved that the same thing happened to all thinking creatures. Summerbreeze shut down the project until shi could figure out what had gone wrong. It took hir nearly two years for hir to determine the problem and find the means of dealing with it. And so was created the mind-matrix, a holographic model of the animal's mind that perfectly mirrored its higher-order thinking abilities. Some people say that it captures their very souls! Please don't ask me how it functions. It's very esoteric even for me. Anyway, tests were restarted, this time including the use of the mind-matrix. To their relief, all the test animals came through utterly normal. Finally it was time to test it on a sapient being. Summerbreeze refused to let anyone else try it, putting responsibility for its success or failure squarely in hir paws. Well, to make a long story short, it worked perfectly and Summer came through whole and heartily relieved. And so was born the matter transporter that we use today."

As Goldfur paused for a moment, I asked, "What happened to Joyleap, do you know?"

"Yes, I do. Hir mind was a blank state, having far less sophistication than even that of a newborn cub who learns even while in the womb. It took months to even get hir back to that level, and then shi had to grow up all over again, except that shi already had an adult's body. It complicated matters a great deal, but eventually shi became a virtually normal chakat again. However, shi was a completely different personality. Everything that had made Joyleap an individual was gone and replaced by a new personality created from different lifetime experiences. Joyleap was officially pronounced dead and the chakat renamed *Nova*, meaning *New*.

"Amazing. It makes me wish I'd learned more about this in school," I commented.

"I'm sure you know some biology-related facts that would make a fascinating story also, but for now, I'd better finish my explanation. After the creation of the body pattern, a matrix of the subject's mind is made, preserving their personality and experiences, and is transmitted to the destination. Only then is their body converted to the plasma state and imposed on a transmission beam and sent to the receiver where the process is reversed. The plasma is injected into a containment field, the matrix is imposed, then the pattern pulls mind and body back together again into the right form. The stasis field holds it all together until the plasma is de-energised and reverts to normal matter. The fields are dropped and *voila*! The subject has been safely transported."

"Hmmm. Couldn't you simply use matter at the other end rather than sending all that mass?" I asked.

"Yes, you could, but it would require the right mix of raw material at the other end. You can't just stick any matter into the process. Besides, you start creating other problems that way. Most sentients wish to have their body back, not something created at the other end. Besides, that leaves open the possibility of producing several perfect clones from the one matrix and pattern. This has been banned on moral grounds. However, it's perfectly okay for non-living things. That's how replicators work. Just shovel in the right raw ingredients and use a stored pattern to re-form it into the desired object, from a filet mignon to a marble statue.

"Why isn't this process used to manufacture everything then?"

"Because it's a far too energy-intensive process. It costs far less to manufacture it the old-fashioned way, but on a starship, it's a lot more practical than carting along everything that you possibly *might* need, so replicating parts is only limited to the number of patterns you can store. Besides, with their antimatter powered engines, they have a lot of spare power at their beck and call. Earth-bound antimatter power plants are considered too dangerous. Unlike a starship, there's nowhere safe to eject the antimatter core, so power generation limitations still exist."

"I see. So this process was interrupted by the explosion? How did Dale end up with a copy of your body?"

"All the data is sent and copied to the receiver's buffer before reintegration is commenced. This way they it can be error-checked and then allows the transmitter to disconnect while the receiver goes through the rematerialisation process. The pattern remains in the buffer until the next incoming one overwrites it. We never received Dale's pattern, so mine was still in the buffer. We had his mind-matrix though. We were close to panicking when we realised we had everything but the pattern. Up until that point, Dale was still technically alive, but we couldn't do anything about it."

"So you used your own pattern to create a body for Dale. Wait a minute! You're far more massive than a human. How did you cope with the problem of all the extra mass you needed?"

"Well done! You've seen the problem that I was faced with. The answer? Sheer bloody luck! You remember what I told you about Dale's baggage? All that organic material contained just enough of the essential ingredients to recreate the entire mass of my body."

"My muttha always sed dat froot wood be good fuh me," Dale murmured. "I don' thin' she had dis in mind tho."

"Well, at least shi's retained some sense of humour," I thought to myself. *"So that's a good sign at least."* Aloud, I said, "It seems the whole event involved a lot of luck."

"You've got a talent for understatement," Goldfur agreed fervently. "If the process had been interrupted at any time other than at the exact moments between receiving the matrix and the pattern, Dale would have had virtually no chance whatsoever. Shi might have been mind-damaged at least, but more likely would have died. The transporter specialists who took the incident report almost couldn't believe that we had achieved what we did, the probability being that small. Even I was amazed. I was grasping at straws when I realised my pattern was still in the buffer and I decided to try it. I didn't have the luxury of time to work it out."

"Why not?"

"For starters, as I've said already, the continuous power drain is enormous and can't be sustained for long, but worse still, the mind-matrix is volatile and will start to break down after a short period."

"Oh! That would cause memory loss at least, or that mind-damage that you mentioned, I suppose?"

Goldfur nodded. "Yeah. That and worse."

"So how did shi react when shi rematerialised?"

Dale suddenly spoke up, hir speech still oddly slurred, but slowly getting better. It was like someone who had come out of a dentist appointment with their mouth numbed by anaesthetic that was slowly wearing off. Taking into account the distortions, what shi said was: "I didn't even realise that anything had gone wrong. I went to step off the transporter pad and stumbled. I threw my hands forward to catch myself and realised two things. First: I wasn't falling forward because a weight behind me was stopping that, and second: those weren't my hands! I stopped and stared at them, then followed the arms up to my torso, my chests, my... breasts?! Looking further, I saw that the rest of me had changed too. I recognised the form as that of a chakat, then I don't remember any more before coming to in the port's sick bay."

"Shi fainted," Goldfur confirmed. "The medics said it was only shock though and otherwise gave hir a clean bill of health."

"Huh! They may have said that I was okay, but I felt awful. At first, I couldn't do anything right. I could hardly even talk. I was too conscious of having a muzzle, a bigger tongue, etcetera. Once the doctor gave me a mild sedative though, I relaxed enough for the body's memory to take over."

"You're still a bit garbled though," I pointed out.

"Some things I'm going to have to re-learn, including talking and walking it seems, and controlling this tail is a totally new skill." Shi shook hir tail's black tip at me, apparently not having relinquished it since I had handed it to hir.

"You sound almost resigned to being a chakat," Goldfur interjected. "You know that the techs will be working on a way to restore you to human form."

Dale's control of hir body might have been incomplete, but the cynical look on hir face was unmistakable as shi replied, "Yeah, sure! You just got through telling us what a colossal fluke it was getting me into this body. What chance have I got of getting back to normal?"

"You shouldn't give up so easily," Goldfur replied sternly. "Attempting that under controlled conditions will be much easier than relying on luck in an emergency. Probably the longest thing will be the time spent testing to ensure that the process will be safe."

Dale looked unconvinced, but said no more. Goldfur looked at hir with concern, then sighed. "Well, one step at a time, I suppose. Just like we've been doing since the accident." Shi turned hir attention back to me. "After Dale had the tranquilliser, the doctor interviewed hir, then booked hir a session with psych division. We tried to get hir walking again, with mixed success, as you found out. Then we went to the duty officer's office where we started debating what to do about hir situation. I belatedly realised that you'd probably be waiting for me by then and had you paged. The commander said that he'd bet that you wouldn't be able to tell me apart from Dale and I contradicted him, so he said he wanted me to prove it and not give away who was who. And that's where you came in."

"Heh! Surprised him, didn't we? Anyway, it still seems a short time spent on Dale's problem."

"It was, admittedly, but the general consensus was that they needed to gather more experts to study the case, and in the meantime I insisted that shi'd be better off with other chakats to consult with problems. I know my body better than anyone else, and I'd best be able to interpret hir needs. And so here we are!"

Indeed, and despite my sister's glib and confident tone, I knew we had quite a task before us. Of course, I didn't need to involve myself, but I was prepared to back my sister in whatever course of action shi chose, just as I knew shi would do for me. We spent what remained of the journey home in quiet contemplation of the situation.

* * *

The 'fun' started all over again when we got home. Midnight, my raven-black furred, blue-eyed chakat lifemate had been cub-sitting in my absence. Although the cub that I was presently bearing was the Admiral's and not hirs, shi still wanted to be present for the birth. Hir presence had been a great help lately, especially to Trina who worked out of a home office and needed a break from child-minding to get on with her architectural work. Lupu frequently did this, but not even the dedicated wolftaur could be available all the time, especially as shi was Goldfur's denmate and therefore usually lived at hir den. I had begun to seriously think of moving into a bigger home so that Goldfur and I could move both our families back in together again. Shi was more than just a sister to me, and I very much missed hir. It was bad enough that shi spent so much time in space, but when shi got home, naturally shi had to devote time to hir mates. A little bit selfishly, I wanted to share more of those times together, but I knew shi felt much the same, so I didn't feel too guilty about it.

Of course, Midnight was just as surprised and confused as I had been to see two of Goldfur, and shi lacked the special bond that Goldfur and I shared. However, shi's very observant and quickly figured out who was who. Eudora, Goldfur's first child by Garrek, had no such problem, bouncing up to hir mother without hesitation. Eudora was getting on to three years of age, but shi had started talking early even for a chakat. Shi informed us in hir childish words and phrases that Lupu had gone out grocery shopping and taken Stonefur with her. It had taken over a year for Lupu to regain the confidence to go out in public without an anxiety attack. Last year, she had visited her old wolf-pack for reasons that she had not fully disclosed to us and had returned with a new determination to overcome her fears. Lately she'd even started taking out her cub without an escort, signalling to us that the mental scars had virtually healed.

The others headed for the living room, Goldfur going on to the kitchen to prepare some tea for all of us. I diverted to the room which Trina used for her office so that I could let her know what was going on and not cause another stir. She didn't even notice me come in, so engrossed was she in her work. My lifemate approached everything with the same intensity, whether it be work, play or sex, and that was one of the secrets to her success. She also liked to work in total comfort and, being an arctic fox, her thick white fur kept her more than warm enough, so she usually worked completely nude, which was perfectly fine in our den as none of us much bothered with clothing in the privacy of our own home. I admired hir gorgeous body for a moment, then quietly padded up behind her and slipped one hand around her to give her a cheeky grope on one breast. She jumped, slapped my hand, then pulled my head down to plant a huge, long kiss on my muzzle. When she was good and ready, she broke it off.

"Hello, Love. Back already?" she asked.

"Already? I'm way overdue! You've been getting too wrapped up in your work again."

"Oh?" She looked at the desk clock. "You're right. So what

happened?"

"Very long story, and one best told all at once to the others at the same time. I just wanted to let you know we were home and to warn you to slip on something. We have a guest."

"Okay. I'll wrap this up and be out there soon. And take this with you..." With that, shi returned my grope, a mischievous look in her eye.

"Mmrrr! Gladly!" I replied with a grin.

When I got back to the living room, Midnight was trying to show Dale some of the place, but shi cut things short when shi realised how much trouble Dale was having just getting about. I heard the kettle whistling and knew that afternoon tea would soon be ready. I was about to suggest that we all settle down on the lounge cushions when the front door opened and Lupu walked in with Stonefur on the cub-leash. She unclipped it and the cub wandered off, heading for the kitchen. Lupu then started to divest herself of the saddlebags full of groceries. She looked a little frazzled.

"Phew! What a scorcher! I sure picked a rotten day to get the shopping bug!"

Indeed, it really was a very hot day although, in the air-conditioned comfort of the PTV and my home, we hardly noticed it. Once she had the saddlebags off, Lupu immediately pulled off the white cut-off T-shirt that she liked to wear. Now, as I said, it was hardly unusual for us to walk about bare-breasted in our own home. It was certainly more comfortable for all of us, especially on days like this. However, it did disconcert Dale who didn't seem to know whether to look away or to pretend not to notice, and ended up simply staring at the wolftaur's beautiful bosom. Lupu then compounded the situation by walking over to give Dale a big, intimate hug and kiss, saying, "I'm glad to have you home, Love. I'm in the mood, if you know what I mean!" Dale was totally flustered now and still couldn't tear hir eyes away. Lupu stepped back, giving hir a lascivious look as if planning her attack. She then continued, "But I see that you are too. Just give me a few minutes to freshen up and I'll be back." With that, she trotted off in the direction of the bathroom.

"But I..." Dale finally forced out belatedly as she disappeared down the hallway. Then shi turned to us accusingly. "Fat lot of help you were!"

"Sorry," I said, "But the situation was priceless." Midnight nodded in agreement and I could see Goldfur smiling from the doorway, chuckling a little as shi cradled Stonefur in hir arms. Obviously the cub hadn't been fooled for a moment either and had made a beeline for hir sire. "Don't let it worry you, dear," I tried to reassure hir. "It's not your fault, and Lupu will laugh off her error. Besides, I think she appreciated your favourable reactions!" The moment I said it, I knew I'd made a mistake. This was not a chakat that I was dealing with, but a human in chakat's fur, and that person was not used to having all their physical reactions visible to all who looked.

"I don't care!" Dale exploded. "Do you think I enjoy walking around like this?" Hir hand made a sweeping gesture, indicating hir still-engorged penis waving in the air. "I've never felt so humiliated! I don't want to have my cock displayed to all who look! I don't want to be feel like a helpless invalid in my own body! I don't want to be stuck in this body at all. I want to be human again! I want... I want..." Shi broke down into incoherent tears, hir body racked with huge gasping sobs. I desperately tried to comfort hir, putting my arms around hir and projecting calmness with my empathic ability. It took a long while, but the outburst finally ceased, although I could still feel the tremors in hir body in the aftermath of the emotional storm. I took hir by the hand and led hir to the lounging rugs. "Our sincere apologies, Dale. We should have known better. Just lie on the rug until you're ready." Shi did so with visible relief. "I can only say that such things are normal to us and we find nothing humiliating about them. True, it can be a trifle embarrassing at inappropriate moments, but I'm sure that you'll quickly learn how to deal with them. As I said, Lupu won't hold it against you; none of us will."

"I know, I know." Dale nodded, calmer now. "It's just one thing piling on top of another. It was one shock too many for one day."

Goldfur walked in with a tray loaded with tea and snacks. "I wish that I could say that it was the last, but it's almost certainly not. My advice is to relax and to learn from each experience. Look at the positive aspects of them," shi said earnestly.

"What positive aspect should I learn from this experience?" Dale asked sceptically.

"Well, as a former human male, I think you'd be pleased to know that your masculine libido is intact," Goldfur offered.

Dale looked slightly startled, then gave hir a crooked smile. "I suppose you're right," shi conceded.

Good, I'll go see Lupu now and explain the situation."

"Thanks. How many more times are we going to go through this?" Dale asked.

I answered, giving my sister a chance to go see Lupu. "A couple more times. My lifemate, Kris, isn't home yet, and Goldfur's lifemates need to be told. Garrek is going to be back soon, in time for my birthing party, but you might not see Malena at all unless we go to her village. Then my mate, Boyce, is going to have to be here for the birth of our cub. He's close to my other sisters too."

"Is that all?"

"There's our younger sister, Quickpaw, but shi's away at college at the moment. Our parents should be informed too, I suppose."

"I've heard about Chakat extended families. I never expected to get such an abrupt and in-depth introduction into one though!" Dale said ruefully.

"I suppose that it can get a bit confusing to those who aren't brought up in such a family, but don't worry, you won't need to deal with most aspects of this. All we need to do for the moment is get you used to your new body. Enough about that for now, let's have this tea while it's fresh." I started pouring some tea for Dale after pushing the tray of cookies in hir direction. Before giving hir the mug, I grabbed a napkin. Handing them both to hir, I cautioned, "Take it easy. Drinking from a mug with a new mouth might be a bit tricky."

Sure enough, Dale did end up dribbling some, but seemed to get the knack eventually. Once shi did though, shi drank it down quickly and asked for more. It occurred to me that neither shi nor my sister had probably found the opportunity to have something to drink for a quite a while. It turned out that another was thirsty too, because Goldfur returned not with just Lupu, but with hir tiny new daughter in hir arms, nursing at hir breast. "I hope this doesn't bother you, Dale," Goldfur said, "But little Tailstalker here woke up mewling for a meal."

Dale shook hir head. "No, that's fine by me. It's hardly the first time I've seen mothers breastfeeding their children."

Goldfur laid down besides the coffee table and grabbed the mug of tea that I had ready for hir and gulped it down. "Aaahhh! I needed that!"

Dale nodded in agreement. "Yes, this is great tea. How did you know how I'd like it?" shi asked me curiously.

I shrugged. "I guessed that if you had Goldie's body, you'd share hir tastes too, so I made it the way shi prefers it."

Dale looked thoughtfully into the depths of hir mug. "Hmmm. If that's true, it might mean that I may have to learn what I like all over again too."

Just then, I heard the rear door open and, moments later, Kris' voice called out, "I'm home!

"In here, Love!" I called back.

"Do I smell tea and cake?" asked my handsome fox lover as he entered the living room. "I'm dying of thirst..." He halted abruptly as he spotted the twin Goldfurs, but before he could say anything more, I spoke up.

"You're just in time for an interesting tale. Chase up Trina and we can satisfy everyone's curiosity. I already called her, but she may have gotten distracted again."

Kris nodded, and eyebrow still cocked quizzically, and headed off to Trina's office. Judging by how quickly she appeared in the doorway, Kris had mentioned Goldfur's double and Trina's curiosity had shot into overdrive. They both joined us immediately. Fortunately Trina had put on some clothing. Of course, her idea of dressing decently left little to the imagination. She wore a small bikini top that showed plenty of cleavage and her nipples prominently poking the fabric. Her shorts were small even before she cut them off. Trina loved to show herself off to her mates, and both Kris and I were very glad of that! She'd long since regained her fine lean form after giving birth to Markus, and was enough to drive any male to distraction. Heaven knows what it was doing to Dale! Goldfur retold the tale of Dale's fate while I, after adding my small part, cleared up the afternoon tea and kept the cubs amused.

After the explanation was completed, Goldfur and the others managed to keep Dale talking, getting to know more about hir and generally keeping hir mind occupied. I noticed a rapid improvement in hir speech too. More of the body memory coming into play, I guessed. At one stage, I got up to order some pizzas. All of us were too wrapped up in the events to be bothered with cooking! We feasted well, and washed them down with copious amounts of soft drink. Of course, the time came when I needed to relieve my bladder because of that, but as I excused myself to go the toilet, Dale tapped on my arm for attention.

"I need to go to the loo also," shi murmured.

I nodded, understanding, or so I thought. I helped hir up and steadied hir once again on the way down the hall to the bathroom. Once there, I pointed out the toilet facilities to Dale. The taur version was still a porcelain flush bowl, but slightly more oval shaped and recessed into the floor where we could squat upon it. The extra length of the bowl and the hooded lip let us urinate easily without splashing. I stood back to let Dale use the facilities first. Shi walked into the cubicle and then just stood there with a helpless look on hir face.

"You can close the door for privacy, you know," I remarked, although I was sure shi would have realised that for hirself. We may walk about nude, but there were some things we preferred doing in private!

"That's not the problem," shi replied.

"Well, what is?" I asked exasperatedly.

"Umm, well, *how* do I piss?"

That floored me. It's something that I never think about. After all, I had done it since I was a kitten, long before I remembered learning how to do so. I had to think a moment. We chakats urinate like a normal male, through our penis, and that meant first extruding it from the sheath. This was quite simple... unless you never had those muscles before and didn't know how to use them! I explained this to Dale and shi made a conscious effort to do so, but failed.

"What am I going to do now? Just let go? I'm ready to burst!"

Thank God shi still had bladder control! "No, you don't want to do that. The urine will make a mess around your belly fur. There's only one thing that I can think of and that's to physically push it out the way we do with cubs we're trying to toilet train."

Dale didn't look too thrilled about that idea, but it wasn't as if shi had much choice and shi mutely nodded agreement. I wasn't overjoyed about it either. I thought a couple of dark thoughts about Goldfur who should've been doing this. After all, it was hir idea to help Dale. Then I sighed, remembering that I had agreed to help without any reservation, then squeezed in next to Dale. The cubicle was normally roomy enough for an adult chakat and a cub, but it was never intended for two adults. I realised this was just as embarrassing for hir as it was for me, so I stopped worrying about it and put my hand on hir sheath, pressuring the penis within to move forward. It took a couple of tries to do it right as it wasn't quite the same as it was for a cub, but then shi was sufficiently exposed and pointed in the right direction. "Let it go now," I told hir. Moments later, with a sigh of relief, shi did.

When shi was done, I released my hold and hir penis slid back into its sheath. Shi stepped out of the cubicle, followed closely by me. "Thank you, Forest. I'm so sorry that I was such a bother."

"Nonsense, Dale. It's hardly your fault. However, I do suggest that you practice that and try to gain control of those muscles. I really don't want to be having to nursemaid you through that too often!"

Dale nodded in fervent agreement, then waited while I took my turn in the loo, then escorted hir back to the table. One more crisis overcome for now. I didn't bring up Dale's problem as it would have been too embarrassing for hir. I'd tell Goldfur about it later, privately. Instead, I steered the conversation towards Dale in an attempt to find out more about our guest.

"Dale, isn't there any family expecting you to turn up?" I asked.

Shi shook hir head. "As I explained to Goldfur back at the spaceport, my family is the pioneering type. They left to become Martian colonists. I chose to stay on Earth when they moved because I'd just completed school and had been accepted into the Star Corps training program. I thought at the time that I'd eventually rejoin my family on Mars, but I never did as I realised that I wanted to keep Earth as my home base. However, my closest relatives live on the other side of the continent, so I don't see them much.

"Sounds a bit lonely," I commented. "Don't you at least have a girlfriend? Or boyfriend," I added.

Dale's inner ears pinked and I realised that I had embarrassed hir inadvertently. "There is a girlfriend," Dale conceded, "Although I don't know what Sharon's going to think of this!" Shi made a broad gesture, starting at the breasts and sweeping down to indicate hir taur body. "I was going to give her a call when I got back. I don't know if I can do that now."

"At the very least, I think she deserves to be told," I advised.

Dale nodded. "I think I'd better get Commander Redfang to pass on that news. I really don't think she'd believe a strange chakat claiming to be her boyfriend."

"You have a point," I said with a small smile. "We'll cross that bridge when we come to it. So, basically what you're saying is that we're the only 'family' that you have for now?"

Dale shrugged. "So it seems. Look, I'm sorry for having been such a sourpuss before..." Hir mouth quirked up briefly as shi realised the pun that shi had just made. "... but I'm grateful for all the help that you've given me." Shi looked at Goldfur. "I think that you were right to insist that I come with you. I reckon that I'm going to learn how to handle this body a lot more quickly with your help." Shi held up hir tail and its tip twitched back and forth instead of just hanging limp as it had been. "I've learned how to do that so far. Hopefully I'll also learn how to hold the whole thing up off the floor soon." Shi put it down again. So, before I lose my temper in frustration again, I want to thank you and Forest for all your efforts." Shi turned to Lupu next. "Thanks for the cuddle. Even if it wasn't meant for me, I think it broke me out of the funk that I was in."

Lupu dropped hir jaw in a big wolfy grin. "There are more like that if you need 'em!"

Dale actually smiled back this time. My word! Lupu must have really put something into that embrace! Then Dale turned to Trina. "I'm sorry if it seems that I have been staring at you a lot this evening. I don't want you to think that I'm just interested in your looks."

Ha! As if! Trina absolutely revelled in attention. She would have been more annoyed if he had <u>not</u> looked!

Dale continued. "You see, you remind me of a girlfriend I had back in the final year of school."

"You had an Arctic Fox vixen as a girlfriend?" I blurted out.

"What's so surprising about that?" Dale asked. "Just because I prefer being a human doesn't mean that I'm humanocentric."

Dale's rebuke stung, but I deserved it. I had jumped to an unwarranted conclusion. After all, I also had a human mate who enjoyed being human. I think that Dale's desperation to have hir old body back must have misled me.

"Anyway," Dale continued, "She wasn't an Arctic Fox but a Red Fox. She was the most gorgeous female in the class, and she could have had any male in the school, but she chose me. And, no, she wasn't just a BBV!"

"Ummm... what's a BBV supposed to be?" Lupu asked.

Goldfur answered, "Literally, it's initial slang for Big Breasted Vixen. What it means is that the female is beautiful but stupid. The modern equivalent of the old-time dumb blondes."

"Oh, I get it. But how did they get that name? I've yet to meet a really stupid vixen."

"That goes back to the times before the Gene Wars," I answered. "Back then, morph species were bred for very selfish reasons. Foxes especially were designed to be sex toys, both female and male. Their beautiful fur made them highly desirable, but nobody wanted their toys to have a mind of their own. Therefore, they were bred to have strong sexual appetites, gorgeous looks and very little brains. The vixens were usually engineered to have very generous breasts, hence the beginning of the BBVs. After the Wars, most of the morph species had been wiped out, but foxes had survived through sheer numbers and their proclivity for breeding. However, the post-war world could not afford to have such useless creatures wasting valuable limited resources, but neither could they just kill them. Instead, one of the goals of places like the newly established Institute of New Generation Genetics was to use genetic engineering to uplift the foxes, and other similarly afflicted species, to a normal level of mental and physical standards. Fixing their intelligence was relatively easy as the old-time gene-engineers had merely placed a neural inhibitor into the brains of their products. Removing that allowed the adults to become a bit smarter, but it also meant that their children were born with a completely normal ability to learn."

"Exactly!" Dale interjected. "Mary-Anne Renelle, my girlfriend, was not only intelligent, she was head of the class!"

"You'll have to tell me more about her," Lupu said.

"I'll do that if you like," Dale replied, then looked a little

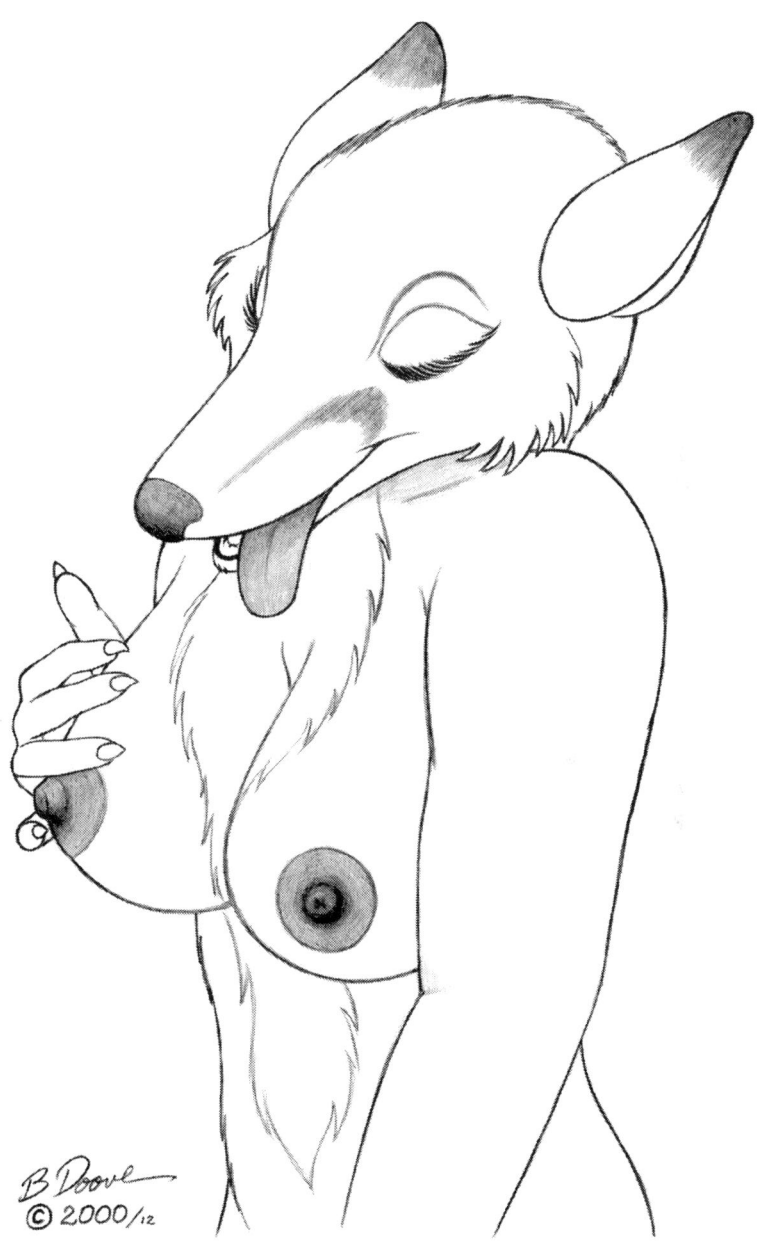

guiltily at me. "But I think I'd better let Forest finish first."

"Thanks," I said dryly. "Anyway, the next step was to do something about their excessive sexual endowments and hyperactive sex-drive. This took longer due to the fact that they were so deeply ingrained into their genetic structure and the gene-engineers were dealing with people with rights rather than lab animals. Gradually though, all the species were brought back to reasonable levels. However, to this day, you will not find a flat-chested adult vixen. That, along with their still strong sexual proclivities, helps maintain the stereotype of the BBV, much to their annoyance." I pulled Trina closer to me and cuddled her. "But I love my lifemate just as she is!"

Trina gave me a lick-kiss and added, "I wouldn't want to have any less of a libido anyway. I enjoy my sex-life just fine, thank you!"

Dale nodded in agreement. "It's true. Mary-Anne had a healthy sex-drive and, after we'd been going out for a while, she was the one who wanted to start sexual relations. We had so much in common besides that though. We both liked the same books, music, movies, food... you name it! Later we found out that we were also very compatible in bed."

"So why didn't you make her your mate then?" Lupu asked.

"We _had_ started thinking about it. Then we graduated. As I said, she was very intelligent. Her scores got her into Star Fleet Academy. I didn't make the cut and went into the Star Corps instead and joined one of their training programs. I still wanted a career in space, you see. A bit of the family pioneering spirit, perhaps. We tried to keep up our relationship, but distance and lack of time made things nearly impossible. Eventually we reluctantly agreed to close our relationship. We both wanted to pursue our careers and I refused to hold Mary-Anne back. I... I still miss her sometimes."

Lupu put her hand on Dale's back and stroked hir gently.

"I'm sorry if I re-opened any unhappy memories, Dale."

"No, Lupu, they were very happy memories, but life goes on. I do have a nice girlfriend now, albeit a human one. She's pleasant company, although she doesn't mean as much to me as Mary-Anne did." Then Dale realised what Lupu was doing and hir ears flushed with blood again. I grinned. It seemed that the wolftaur had taken a shine to our visitor. I hoped that Dale was up to her attentions!

There were a few quiet introspective moments during which we sipped our tea, trying to unwind. Despite the wide-rimmed mugs, Dale was still having some difficulty drinking the hot beverage, but refused any more help. It was best that shi got as much practice as possible anyway. However, while watching hir discreetly, I realised that shi was shifting about uncomfortably, then furtively rubbing hir breasts. I suspected that shi wasn't telling us something, so I decided to try to draw it out of hir.

"Dale, is something wrong? You look bothered by something." Again, Dale flushed, hir ears nearly glowing in embarrassment, but shi mutely nodded. "Spit it out!" I insisted.

Dale gave a sigh of resignation, then put hir hands on hir breasts. "Are these supposed to ache so much? It's been getting steadily worse since I first noticed it about dinner time."

"Uh-oh," Goldfur said. "I should have thought of that possibility earlier."

"Is it bad?" Dale asked worriedly.

"Not exactly," my sister replied. "As you've seen, I'm a nursing mother, and now so are you! Your breasts are overfull with milk. You will need to get rid of a lot of it or else the pain will just keep getting worse. We can go about half a day between feeds, and I nursed Tailstalker just before I left for work, and again when I got home, but you've gone several hours past that time. No wonder you're feeling uncomfortable!"

"You mean I have to breastfeed cubs now?" Dale asked with a touch of horror in hir voice.

"Well, that's the best and most obvious solution," Goldfur conceded, "But it's not the only one. However, I guess you won't like the alternative much either."

"And that is...?" Dale asked apprehensively.

Goldfur continued, "Well, I have another cub by another mate who lives in California. Malena is a foxtaur vixen, and because chakat kittens need certain trace nutrients that aren't present in foxtaur milk, I needed to supply some of my own to supplement the cub's diet. Therefore I regularly used a breast pump to extract the milk to send to Malena to feed to our child. I propose that we relieve you of your milk burden in the same way, unless you'd prefer to nurse a cub, of course."

Dale threw up hir hands in denial. "No, no thanks! But isn't there another alternative?"

Goldfur looked at me questioningly. As a biologist, I knew a few more things about this than shi did, but I shook my head and answered, "None that we know about. After all, stopping lactation has never been a need for us, only starting it."

"You mean that I'm going to be producing milk forever if I'm stuck this way?" Dale asked, desperation creeping into hir voice.

"No, no!" I hastened to reassure hir. "When the cubs are about a year or so old, we start the weaning process, gradually reducing the amount we feed the cub until lactation ceases of its own accord. We'll just artificially start the weaning process immediately."

Dale looked relieved. "I suppose that's a lot better than the alternative. How many days will it take?"

"Well, I think we're talking weeks, even months maybe. That's the normal natural rate." I saw Dale begin to panic again and before shi could speak up, I added a little testily, "Look! This has never had to be done before, and we weren't designed to be turned off like a tap. Unless the med-techs can suggest a better, safe alternative, you're just going to have to put up with the inconvenience. And if you're worried about looking silly, grow up! It's a perfectly natural function and nothing to be ashamed about." I stopped myself. I was annoyed that I had lost my temper even that much. "Sorry Dale, I didn't mean to snap at you."

"It's okay Forest. I think I needed that verbal slap in the face. I suppose it would be best to get this over with now. At least I can avoid further discomfort. What do I need to do?"

Suddenly Lupu spoke up. "I'll help you with that, Dale. I've helped Goldfur sometimes and I know the procedure."

I saw Goldfur give hir den-mate a surprised glance. We both knew the sort of 'help' that Lupu usually gave, although I doubted that she intended to do that this time. No, for some reason, Lupu seemed to have taken an intense interest in her mate's clone. I sensed Goldfur's mental shrug. It was Lupu's business, and if she wanted to do this, neither of us could think of a reason why she should not. Lupu seemed like an excited puppy as she helped Dale up and escorted her to the kitchen. Well, where else would you store milk? I started tidying up the plates, mugs and the remains of the pizzas, putting them onto a tray to take into the kitchen when the two were finished. In the meantime, we'd give Dale some privacy until shi got used to having to do this. I heard Goldfur sigh and I raised an eyebrow questioningly at hir. Shi shook hir head.

"I don't know what Lupu is up to any more than you do. Since she came back from that trip to visit her old pack last year, things have been slowly changing."

"Changing? How so?"

"Oh, she's still affectionate and caring for the cubs, but she's also been broody and I can sense her general feeling of dissatisfaction and frustration."

"She's even been acting territorial around me sometimes," Trina put in. "Although she apologises for that later."

"Do you think that she's pining for her true family, maybe?" Midnight asked.

"That would be my guess," Goldfur replied, "Or at least a part of it. Let's face it: sometimes what she does and how she thinks is completely alien to me. It was Forest who pointed out to me how she regarded my family as her substitute pack and me as pack alpha, but what else had I overlooked? I did a bit of research into wolf behaviour. Did you know that while wolf cubs are watched over by the entire pack, a few members specifically look after them? That's essentially been Lupu's role for a while. I never tried to pry into her past, but I get the impression that she had some rank previously, whereas with me, she has to settle for third place behind Garrek and Malena. Maybe she wants more? Maybe she isn't satisfied with being just a child-carer anymore?"

"And maybe we're reading too much into the comparisons between wolves and wolftaurs. Perhaps something about Dale's personality intrigues her?" Midnight speculated.

"Then we're back to square one," Trina commented.

"Uh-huh. I think we'd better let this one play out for a little longer and see what happens," Midnight recommended.

We all nodded in agreement, then we continued conversing about more immediate problems.

"You do realise that if Dale is going to have that much of a problem with mere breastfeeding, shi's going to absolutely freak out when shi goes into heat?" I asked.

Goldfur glumly nodded. "Yeah, I'd already realised that. We'd better lay in some stocks of the suppression herbs."

"You got that right," I fervently agreed. "How long before you next go into heat?"

"The day after tomorrow."

"Hooboy! That doesn't give hir much time to adapt, or for us to prepare!" Trina exclaimed.

"No, it sure doesn't..."

Just then, the comm started ringing insistently. I walked over to answer it, then called Goldfur over when I recognised Commander Redfang on the screen.

"How are things going, Shir Goldfur?" he started conversationally.

"As well as can be expected, sir," shi answered.

"Good!" The niceties over, he continued, "There will be a few visitors coming over to your place tomorrow to see Ensign Perkins. One is that psych specialist with whom we booked a session, so Perkins won't have to come into headquarters for that. He will make a preliminary assessment as to how the ensign is coping. A couple of transporter and medical specialists want to poke and prod the poor fellow a bit more and ask a few more questions. I don't know if they're going to learn anything useful, but we've promised to try. They wanted him... hir... to come into one of the research laboratories, but I've left that up to the psych specialist to determine. She may say that Perkins is better off staying with you for the moment, as you've already said. Anyway, because of this, you won't be reporting here tomorrow. Your current responsibility is the ensign's welfare until further notice." He grimaced a bit. "Not that you could do much here anyway. The space station is under security lockdown by Star Fleet until they give it a very thorough check for other possible sabotage and investigate this incident. Very limited access is being allowed through shuttles and the transporters of the *Archimedes* which is still docked to the station, but that precludes you for now."

"Understood," Goldfur replied. "Sir, do you know more about the incident yet?"

The commander hesitated, then made up his mind. "Keep this to yourself for now. The news will be released to the press tomorrow when we have more information to go with it. We got a message from some group claiming responsibility for the disaster, quoting details that aren't generally known to support their claim, so we believe it's genuine. While they didn't give a name, they espoused all the tenets of the *Humans First* fanatics, demanding that the Star Corps starts removing all morph species from the organisation or else more 'accidents' would start happening."

The choice of the Star Corps as a target hardly surprised me. It was one of the greatest employers of morph species due to the fact that it had need of the talents of the various species. Once upon a time, soon after the Gene Wars, Earth had had the need for these talents, but once civilisation had been put back onto its feet again, this need had diminished. Space was the new frontier though, and both Star Fleet and the Star Corps were common goals for many morph species who wanted to make the most of their abilities. Eliminating morphs from either organisation was clearly ridiculous though as some filled roles that no human could fill quite as well, and the number of personnel lost would cripple both branches of the Star Services.

"Gentlefurs," Redfang continued, "I believe we have witnessed the beginning of the escalation from lunatic cult to outright terrorists."

"As if the death of my child wasn't enough evidence," Goldfur muttered to hirself.

"What was that?" the Commander asked.

"Nothing. Thanks for the update, sir."

He nodded. "Report by comm after the specialists leave. And good luck with Ensign Perkins." He cut the connection.

I turned to my sister. The report had re-opened an old wound and I could feel hir sense of loss renewed. I put my arm around hir and nuzzled hir. Shi smiled at me, patted my hand and pushed the hurt aside. We made our way back to the lounge cushions where we quietly snuggled for a while. The others sensed the mood and excused themselves, taking the cubs with them. Eventually Lupu emerged from the kitchen, carefully guiding Dale out with her. Dale plonked down ungracefully and then Lupu followed suit, settling down close beside hir.

"Mission accomplished!" she said with a grin.

"Good," I said. "How did it go, Dale?"

"Well, after getting over feeling extremely silly, it went pretty well. God! I could hardly believe how much milk these things produced!" Shi said this as stared down at hir breasts. "The sensation was... not unpleasant."

I gave a purring laugh. "Now there's an understatement! No, don't get embarrassed again. You just touched on one of my favourite subjects," I said with a reassuring grin.

"One of Lupu's too, I suspect," replied Dale with a glance at the wolftaur. Lupu just put on an innocent face, but couldn't hold it and broke into her wolfy grin again.

"Chakat cubs, having large taur bodies, have quite an appetite, so it's hardly surprising we produce a lot of milk to feed them. Anyway, we'll measure how much milk you produced and start the tapering off process tomorrow. The sooner we start the weaning process, the sooner we'll get results.

"Amen!" said Dale, then yawned hugely. The evening was

still early, but this had to have been a stressful and very tiring experience. I caught Goldfur's eye and shi nodded. We both got up and helped Dale to hir feet. "Come, Dale," I said, "It's time you got some sleep. You can rest up for as long as you like. Tomorrow isn't going to be easy for any of us."

Dale mutely agreed and let hirself be led to the spare sleeping den. "Make yourself comfortable, dear," I said, indicating the huge soft mattress we used instead of a bed. "Don't fret about anything. We'll call you when we think that you've slept long enough, or if someone calls for you."

"Thanks," shi replied. "Umm, where are the blankets?"

Goldfur and I grinned. My sister replied, "You've got a fur coat, dear. You don't need blankets!"

Shi looked startled, then grinned back sheepishly. "Okay, but can I keep wearing this T-shirt? I don't think that I'd feel right sleeping completely nude."

"Sure! Whatever makes you comfy."

Shi smiled gratefully. "Thanks again."

"You're welcome, Dale." Goldfur then turned and left the room.

I stayed a bit longer and watched as Dale tried to make hirself comfortable, then turned to follow my sister. I paused at the doorway and turned back to face Dale, and asked hesitantly, "Do you want company for the night, dear?"

Again shi was surprised momentarily, but then a slight smile replaced that. "Thanks, but no. I think I'll be alright, and I don't think I'm ready for the famous chakat communal bed just yet."

I smiled back. "Very well, but don't hesitate to ask us for

anything if you need it. Goodnight Dale." I dimmed the light, then closed the door behind me. I rejoined Goldfur, suddenly more grateful than ever to have my family there to share my life, it's trials and triumphs both. Dale's problems made mine seem small in comparison. Still, I had to wonder how much more trouble our transmogrified friend would cause in hir efforts to rebuild hir life. And what sort of a life would it be? Despite hir cooperation with teaching hir how to deal with hir new body, shi still did not regard hirself as a chakat, and that I found to be faintly disturbing. I had a clear image of who and what I was, but Dale's had been ruthlessly ripped apart. How could we guide hir to create a new self-image if shi could not deal with *what* shi was?

PART TWO
Learning About Oneself

Dale woke from a marvellous dream, one of those that you can't really remember but know that everything is just perfect. He stretched languorously, all limbs extended, getting the kinks out after a long sleep. It felt so pleasant to just take his time and feel his body awaken. He took the time to take pleasure in the sensation of curling his fingers and toes, claws fully extended, stretching his arms, his forelegs, hind legs... *HIND LEGS*???!!!

Dale's eyes flew open; a half-strangled yelp coming from his throat before the memories of the previous day's events came back to him. His hearts thumping, he breathed deeply, trying to regain self-control. After about a minute, he started taking stock of himself. No, he hadn't dreamed about the accident that had befallen him. This wasn't even a nightmare. This was a very harsh reality. Yes, he was still trapped in the unfamiliar body of a chakat. Then he remembered the stretch and how, for a few brief seconds, he could feel every part of his new form, and *knew* with a strange impossible familiarity where everything was and how it worked. He attempted to get up and half-succeeded. Unfortunately, that fleeting knowledge had not miraculously given him the ability to cope with his new form, but it did seem to have helped a bit. He closed his eyes and tried to recapture those moments of stretching and how the muscles felt as he used them. He then tried again, this time getting to all fours with almost creditable smoothness.

"Another step in the right direction," he murmured to himself. "I'll get used to this yet!" He straightened out the T-shirt he was still wearing, grunting in resignation at the sight and feel of his breasts restricting the movement. Then his long hair fell in front of his eyes and he grabbed a brush from the chest of drawers next to the bed and tried to tame it, grumbling and wondering why

anyone would want to put up with hair that was waist-long. As he was doing so, he caught sight of his reflection. A full-length mirror adorned the door of the wardrobe and Dale could not resist the urge to look at himself. It wasn't as if he didn't know what he looked like because he was now Goldfur's exact double, but looking at *hir* just wasn't the same. He took his time examining the new form that an amazing accident had bestowed upon him. A cougar taur stared back at him from the mirror. The lower torso was that of a powerfully built feline, not too different from that of one of the big hunting cats, although a little longer in the legs. The tail was exceptionally long though, and prehensile as well. Dale waved it a bit, proud of his mastery of that little feat. The paws on the forelegs had exceptionally long digits, capable of acting as another pair of strong, though crude, hands. The upper torso was very humanoid in shape, although still covered in the dense golden brown fur that gave his doppelganger hir name. The upper torso was joined to the lower torso at about where the neck should otherwise be. The head was plainly feline, with a broad, powerful muzzle full of dangerous-looking teeth, and above the muzzle was a pretty pair of bright gold-green eyes. The whole lot was topped with human-like light golden hair which he was forced to admit looked really attractive at that length. All up, it was a very good-looking body, but one thing kept making him uncomfortable. Or should he say two things? He pulled off the T-shirt, put his hands on the generously sized breasts and hefted them a little. They were very firm and he judged that they were also very milk-filled, in need of emptying once again. Any female would be proud to have these breasts, although Dale's preferences tended towards a size smaller. The problem was that Dale *wasn't* a female. Until yesterday, he had been an average human male quite satisfied with his current body. Now he was stuck with a new form, one that had the wrong sexual equipment, the wrong number of limbs, and the wrong reflexes to use them.

Dale suddenly realised that he was still staring at his tits, startled to find that he was turning himself on! He dropped his hands and tore his eyes off the image before him. However, the stirring in his loins was not so easily quelled. He tried to clear his mind but it seemed chakat bodies were even more sexually responsive than humans and he had no real success, so instead he gave up and decided to check this out properly while he had privacy. "Well, Forest *did* say to look at the more positive aspects of the situation, so let's see what I'm like in the male department." He manoeuvred himself in front of the mirror then, with some difficulty, lifted the hind leg nearest to his reflection. The sight that greeted his eyes made him gasp. His penis had quickly swollen and slid out of its sheath, once again in plain sight. This time though, he could see it, not just feel it. He had not realised that chakats were so... *large*! The exposed shaft was very human-like despite being adapted for a sheath, only a little longer than the average human's, but it was at least half again as thick. "Must be in proportion to their larger body mass, I suppose," he said wonderingly. He sure didn't feel short-changed with *this* studly cock! For the first time since getting this body, he felt good about something. "I think that ought to please the ladies," he said confidently.

"I know that it's given *me* a good deal of pleasure," came a husky female voice from behind him.

Dale whirled around, mortified at having been caught out like that. He saw the lean form of a female wolftaur, Lupu, leaning against the doorway, grinning ear to ear. "How long have you been there?" he demanded.

"Long enough to see you get all excited and put on a show for me," Lupu replied, a small smirk on her face. That expression was instantly wiped from her face as the hairbrush hurtled at her and she had to duck to avoid it.

"GET OUT!" Dale roared at her, his shame, uncertainty and fear all combining to crack his self-control.

"But, I just..." Lupu tried to begin, then beat a hasty retreat as she saw him reach for the bed lamp. She closed the door protectively behind her and Dale just stood there staring at it for several long seconds, the lamp still in his hand. Then with a cry of anguish, he threw it aside and collapsed onto the mattress and started bawling in huge, racking sobs.

* * *

Both Forestwalker and Goldfur came bounding up to Dale's bedroom, only to be stopped by Lupu. "What's going on in there?" demanded Goldfur.

"I made a bad mistake," Lupu admitted. "I think it's best if we just leave Dale alone for a little while. Please let me deal with this. I want to try to undo my blunder."

Forestwalker said, "Shi's radiating enough misery to upset any chakat within range. You'd better get hir calmed down soon."

"I know! I know! I think Dale just needs to get all this out of his system. He was very restrained last night, but it's only just really hit him this morning. I triggered it off with my ill-timed arrival and words, but I reckon that he'll be ready to listen again soon."

The chakats noticed how Lupu kept referring to Dale as '*he*' while they had continued to use the herm pronouns. Both wondered about this but neither could think of a reason for her to stop doing so. Goldfur nodded to Lupu. "Okay, but remember that shi has to see some Star Corps people today and shi needs to be ready for their arrival. I don't think it will be very productive if shi spends all hir time crying and moping. We need to get hir feeling better about hir situation."

"I know that, Goldie. It's not exactly easy though. Give me some time and I think I can manage though," Lupu said determinedly.

Goldfur was about to add something more when Forestwalker put a hand on hir arm. A moment of understanding passed between them, then Forest said, "Go for it, Lupu. Call us if you need help, but we'll leave him with you for now."

Lupu smiled gratefully. "Thanks! You won't be sorry."

It was another twenty minutes though before Lupu timidly knocked on Dale's door. By now, Dale had cried himself out and was merely wallowing in self-pity. He was completely uncaring about anything and he barely roused himself out of his apathy long enough to say "Come in!" just so the annoying knocking would stop.

Lupu peered cautiously inside, then entered when she realised that she wasn't going to be assaulted. Stopping by the bedding, she gave Dale an appraising look, then said, "I'm very sorry, Dale. I realise now that I made a mistake. I keep forgetting that you're basically still human, despite your body, and you aren't used to our informal ways. Or my blunt manner either."

Dale merely grunted, barely acknowledging her words. Lupu decided that at least he didn't seem likely to throw another fit, so she persisted. "It hadn't been my intention to spy on you, so what I saw was completely accidental. However, it's not as if I haven't seen it all before many times. It's just your innocent reaction to it all that fascinated me. Believe me, you have nothing to be ashamed of. If I had a new body, I'd want to explore it too."

Just when Lupu was about to give up on expecting a reply, Dale murmured, "Why did you come, Lupu? I was expecting to be left in peace until I was ready."

Lupu was relieved. "We *have* left you in peace! You've been asleep for nearly twelve hours and slept half the morning away. I just came by to see if you'd woken yet, and I arrived just as you... well, you know. I should have knocked; I realise that now. I'm just too used to moving freely throughout the den without having to worry about that sort of thing." A loud gurgling from Dale's stomach interrupted Lupu. "I was supposed to tell you that it's the last chance to grab breakfast. I don't think I need to ask if you're hungry.

Again Dale remained quiet for a long period before he

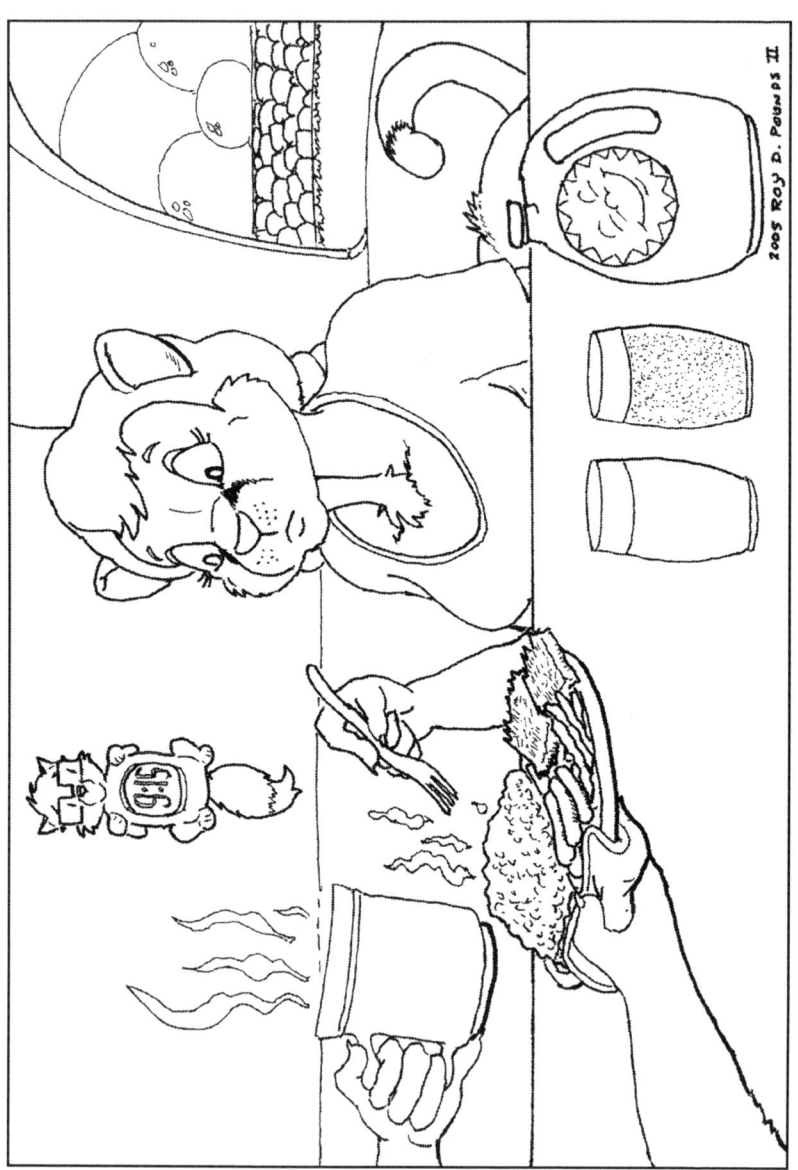

replied. "It seems my body is going to fight me even over this. *Sigh* What about the... er... milk situation?"

Lupu held up the box she had under her arm. "I thought of that. The breast pump equipment is in here. Set yourself up like we did last night. I'm sure you can manage by yourself, so I'll let you have the privacy you need. In the meantime, I'll arrange some breakfast for you." With that, Lupu trotted out of the room, leaving Dale distracted by the task of relieving himself of the mother's milk his breasts had produced overnight. Lupu knew that there would have to be more work done to get Dale back into a positive frame of mind, but at least this was a start.

When Dale finally showed up in the kitchen, Lupu had his breakfast ready. "Park your butt at the table and I'll serve you a meal to keep you going all day!" she said with a smile and served up a huge helping of scrambled eggs on toast with plenty of bacon and a large mug of tea to help wash it down.

"I can't possibly eat all that!" Dale protested, then surprised himself by finishing it all quite easily, feeling the better for it.

Lupu noticed that Dale seemed to have far less difficulty getting about this morning and was pleased that he seemed to be adapting. She was also relieved that he seemed to have gotten over the worst of his attack of depression. She speculated that it might be his chakat physiology influencing him. She took away the dirty plates and cutlery, then sat down next to Dale. "I want to say again how sorry I am for the incident in your room. I never intended to cause you any embarrassment. In fact, I'd like to get to know you a bit better."

Dale quirked an eyebrow at her. "Why?" he simply asked.

Lupu looked a little disconcerted. "I'm not really sure. I mean, I'm a pretty sociable person normally, but I find you in particular rather interesting."

"Not often you get a freak like me, hey?"

"No! That's not what I meant. Dale, I admit that your resemblance to Goldfur has something to do with it, but I've felt something more than that since I gave you that hug yesterday, before I knew who you were. I mean, it was like something lit up inside of me. Why do you think I've been trying to help you so much?"

Dale couldn't think of an answer to that, so he just shook his head.

Lupu snorted exasperatedly. "Oh, come on! Surely you felt something?"

"You mean aside from getting an erection?"

"Of course I mean aside from that! Oh, forget it!" Lupu felt frustrated. She wanted to get to know a little bit more about Dale's background so that she could help him. She also found herself drawn to him in a way that she had only experienced with Goldfur before, something that disconcerted her because she didn't know the reason why. She was racking her brains for another way to approach the subject when Goldfur entered the room with Stonefur in tow.

"Good morning, sleepyhead!" shi greeted hir guest brightly. I hope you're feeling better now, taking present circumstances into account?"

"I'm feeling fine, I guess," Dale replied. "Ummm, what do I do with this?" he asked, holding up the container of milk he'd recently relieved himself of.

"Put it in the fridge to cool, of course." Goldfur took the jug from Dale's hands and did just that, pulling out another similar one and pouring the contents into a mug, then handing it to hir cub. Stonefur started drinking it thirstily.

Dale stared, then stuttered, "You... you mean... that's... *my* milk shi's drinking?"

Goldfur looked at him curiously. "Of course! You don't think we tipped out good milk, do you? We certainly don't buy cow's milk when fresh chakat milk is available. Not only is it tastier, but it's better for cubs than cow's milk."

Dale gaped, his mind a mass of confused emotions. He couldn't refute Goldfur's logic, but even so he found it very hard to accept the concept of children drinking milk that had come from his body.

Goldfur sensed his state of mind and tried to allay his worries. "I suppose I should have realised that you might not have expected that, but providing our spare milk to the cubs is completely normal for us. If I wasn't nursing a cub already, I'd be feeding that to any of the other older cubs too. Don't let your unfamiliarity with your new body and our customs disturb you. It's a completely natural thing. Heck, even humans do that!"

Dale forced a grin. "You're right of course, but I'm going to get this weird picture in my mind every time I empty these things," he said, indicating his breasts. He then took his mind off the subject and concentrated on finishing his mug of tea instead. Goldfur wisely decided that the subject was closed and moved on with the task shi was doing before the incident. When Dale was finished, he leaned back on his haunches with a sigh of satisfaction.

Lupu was about to try initiating a conversation again when the comm started beeping. With a sigh of resignation, she went to answer it. Dale could hear her speaking with another female voice which sounded familiar and he got up and started heading for the comm, only to be met halfway by Lupu with a troubled look on her face. "It's your girlfriend, Sharon. She was informed about your accident and now wants to talk with you."

Dale was both eager and hesitant to talk to Sharon. He

enjoyed spending time with her when he was in port, but frankly didn't know how she was going to take his present circumstances. Still, just standing there wasn't going to help him, so he went to the comm to talk with her. He recognised her image on the screen before she realised that the approaching chakat was going to be talking to her. "Hello, Sharon. It's good to see you."

"Dale?" she asked incredulously.

"In the transformed flesh, believe it or not. I know it's hard to comprehend, but underneath this fur is the same Dale that you've always known."

Sharon looked shaken. After a long pause, she said, "The people at the Star Corps had told me that you had been in a transporter accident and been transformed, but I didn't quite believe them until now. I'm still having difficulty believing." Her expression looked strained, repressing feelings that this situation evoked.

Dale looked grim. "If that's how you feel, think how this must be affecting me. I've been swept up in events since it happened yesterday. I'm glad to see a familiar face at last. Do you think you can come over and talk for a while?"

Sharon's mouth opened as if to say something, but then she just stood there, a panicked look on her face. After a lengthy interlude where Dale was beginning to think that she wasn't going to say anything, she started shaking her head in denial. "No. No, I just can't deal with this. My Dale is a human, not this *furry* pretending to be him!"

Stunned, Dale began to protest, "But it *is* me! I can prove it. Ask me anything!"

"NO! I don't care what you say! Even if part of you was once Dale, you're not my boyfriend now! You don't think I'm going out with a *freak* like you, do you? Don't call me again!" With that, Sharon switched off, leaving Dale staring at a 'Caller has disconnected' message.

Dale just stood there, absolutely shocked to the core. His mind refused to work. He had seen a potential island of stability, only to have it disappear forever. The word '*freak*' echoed through his thoughts over and over again. He stood rooted to the spot until finally Lupu came over and switched off the comm's screen. It was like turning off Dale also. He sank to the floor in shock. Lupu settled down next to him and drew him into a consoling hug. Without even thinking about it, Dale allowed himself to be gathered in her arms. After a short time, she felt the tears begin and silent sobs made his body shudder. Lupu waited until she felt the crying ease up before attempting to say anything.

"Forgive me if I seem to have been eavesdropping, Dale, but I couldn't help but hear what happened. We wolftaurs have good hearing, you know. I didn't know your girlfriend was a furphobe."

"Neither did I... until now," Dale eventually replied.

Encouraged that he was at least responding, Lupu persisted to try to draw him out of his misery and deal with his setback. "You didn't realise this after going with her for several months? How couldn't you? From the moment that I answered the comm, her attitude struck me like that."

"Don't you see? After losing Mary-Anne to Star Fleet, I wanted to have someone as normal as possible, someone who wouldn't give a damn if I worked in space. Someone who wouldn't remind me of Mary-Anne. I never brought up my past, and avoiding any reminder of it was okay by me. I didn't realise that she was avoiding morphs for any other reason simply because I didn't *want* to see!"

"I'm sorry that this had to happen right now, just when you most needed someone at your side. I can help you there, if you'll let me," Lupu said earnestly.

Dale shrugged his shoulders uncaringly. "Why not? Things can't get much worse from here. What did you have in mind?"

Lupu surged to her feet and began to tug Dale to his too. "Nothing fancy. I just want to talk. Get to know the real Dale."

"Didn't I tell you enough last night?" he asked.

"Humph! I heard mostly about your *travels*. I don't want a travelogue; I want a biography!"

"Is that all?" he asked sarcastically, then shook his head. "Sorry, I didn't mean that. Okay, if that's what you want, I'll see what I can do to cure your curiosity. You sure you don't have any feline blood in you?" He gave her a quizzical look, arching an eyebrow.

"Curious as a cat, you reckon? No, but I'm a female, the next best thing!" Lupu grinned broadly at him.

Dale almost smiled at that and allowed himself to be led off to the living room where Lupu parked him on a lounging rug, then settled down in front of him. "Where do you want me to start?" he asked.

"Oh... tell me about your parents and your teenage years."

"That's going way back. Oh well, if that's what you want. My parents have farming in their veins. They grew wheat and other grain on a very large property in New South Wales. Aside from the occasional drought, they did very well and we never lacked for anything. They had only two children, and I'm the younger of two boys. My brother, Nick, was a chip off the old block and took to farming enthusiastically, whereas I was a bit of a dreamer and wanted to travel. I had the exploring bug and would spend hours looking into every corner of our property. When I wasn't out in the fields, I had my nose in a book, looking up some peculiar insect that I found, or an interesting rock."

"So your career with the Star Corps basically started as a childhood hobby?"

"Yeah, I suppose so. Anyway, I certainly wasn't much interested in the farming. I knew that Nick would inherit the farm, not just because he was the eldest, but because that lifestyle was in his blood but not in mine. As I got older, I got more and more dissatisfied with the small town life. It was my relationship with Mary-Anne that helped me through those days. We found that we shared the same interests in discovering things, trying to find out what they were and whether they were useful. She saved me from getting bored out of my mind, and later she confessed that I did the same for her. You can gather that the social life in that small township was pretty much non-existent."

"Obviously! But didn't you do some more typically boy/girl stuff? You couldn't have been a pair of bookworms, could you?"

"Hell, no! She liked traipsing over the countryside with me, but we also liked to spend time playing our music collections. For some reason she liked the old late twentieth century stuff, and it wasn't long before I acquired a taste for it too. Ever hear of *Dire Straits*, Eric Clapton, or *The Rolling Stones*?"

Lupu shrugged helplessly, totally ignorant of what he was talking about.

Dale looked slightly disappointed. "I suppose it's an acquired taste. Anyway, we'd also go out to the movies, go out to restaurants together, and other stuff that lovers might do. Her departure to Star Fleet Academy was a huge blow to me. The last straw though was when my parents announced that they were leaving the farm in the hands of Nick and going to Mars to join the colony there. They were always eager for a challenge. I just hadn't realised that they would go for such a big one! However, while I wanted to see Mars, I didn't want to live there."

"Didn't your parents consult you on that decision? Or did they just shove it on you?"

"Oh, they'd mentioned the possibility before, but I'd never taken it seriously. It stunned me when it was clear that they weren't kidding. When I asked them what they expected me to do, they basically told me that I was old enough to make my own decisions and choose my own path. Seeing as I couldn't join Mary-Anne at the Academy though, I chose the Star Corps as a means of achieving my goals. I trained as a planetary surveyor, a job that required a broad range of skills rather than the specialist ones that required the higher marks that would have gotten me into Star Fleet. Since I graduated, I've been flitting around the stars and seeing what I can see. I love being out in the field, and I have even lived off the land in a few places. Not too unlike your wolftaur pack, I suppose, though there are times when I wished I could have had your fur to keep me warm!"

Lupu grinned at this. "I can imagine. Humans are so vulnerable! You know, you're much better equipped now to spend life on the move. In fact, you'd probably fit in well in a pack."

Dale grimaced. "Maybe so, but it hasn't exactly been in my plans. Anyway, I visit my parents occasionally, but I base myself in a small house on the outskirts of the suburbs. I suppose growing up on the farm made me prefer having elbow-room. I met Sharon fairly recently on one of my shore leaves. She helped fill that void left by Mary-Anne, but obviously I never really got to know her too well. The rest of my life story is pretty dull though, aside from the travel adventures that I told you about last night. Would you like me to tell you about a few more of those?"

"Perhaps later. I find it hard to believe that your life can be summed up in so few sentences though."

"I already said that I my life was pretty dull. Why don't you tell me about yourself instead? How did a wolftaur, a species renowned for mostly living in packs isolated from almost everyone, end up being part of a chakat family?"

Lupu was a bit startled. She hadn't anticipated him turning the tables on her. She was a private person and didn't talk about her past too much. After thinking about it for a moment though, she decided to tell him. "I've not told all these details to everyone, but I think I can trust you, and you deserve to know after telling me about yourself. I'm the youngest of three daughters born to the alpha male and female of my pack, the Eshcranel. While that didn't automatically give us a greater status amongst the pack, it was still quite an advantage."

"Don't you have any brothers?" Dale asked curiously.

"Oh yes, I have three of them. However, they don't have a significant role in what I'm about to tell you. My oldest sister, Clelna, earned her status, and was looking likely to be a successor to the alpha female, our mother, when she stepped down. That would not be for a long while yet, but in the meantime Clelna honed her hunting and leadership skills. I was not the hunting type, but I had learned a few skills that were valuable about the pack. I especially liked working with the leather that the hunters provided from the skins of their kills. I was popular amongst the other members of the pack and was content to take my place behind my oldest sister. Our middle sister though, although a reasonably good hunter, did not enjoy the same popularity. Umfay seemed to delight in gaining advantage by cunning or trickery, rather than more straightforward methods. She had her adherents also, but she would never be popular enough to displace us. It seemed that our destinies were pretty much written. Then one day, Clelna was found dead. That it was murder was never in doubt because they even found the weapon, conveniently left next to the corpse. It was a knife, one that I used for my leatherwork. Of course, that threw suspicion directly onto me."

Dale looked shocked. "The pack thought you were trying to gain the top spot by assassination?"

Lupu nodded glumly. "Yes, that was the first thing some

of them thought of, yet many realised that I simply did not have this ambition. And also, the knife was circumstantial evidence. Anyone could have taken and used it. A few precautions to avoid having their scent on it, and the strong smells associated with working with leather would drown out any other scents but that of the person who used it constantly – me. Of course, some people thought of the possibility of Umfay having done the deed, especially considering her nature, but she had a number of people to give her an alibi, while I did not. My father was forced into the unenviable position of having to judge me. His decision was that there was insufficient evidence to blame me for the murder, but inevitably this still weakened his position with the pack. Some felt he was too lenient because I was his daughter. Others had already condemned me on the strength of the use of my knife alone. My life was ruined either way. I was too young yet to have much authority, my status was compromised, and trust in me had dropped considerably. My life in the pack became miserable. Eventually I chose to leave rather than endure the taunts and accusations."

"Wait a minute!" Dale interjected. "Isn't it obvious that this was all planned? With your sister dead, your status destroyed, and the alpha male's position compromised, that could cause a leadership spill."

"Of course. It shouldn't be a surprise to you that one young ambitious male with high ranking was one of my sister's supporters. If he could wrest the control of the pack from my father, he'd become alpha male, and Umfay could become alpha female."

"Then what happened? Why are you here now? Why wasn't Umfay hounded as badly?"

"You don't fully understand wolftaurs. We're always jockeying for position within the pack. Members are always striving to increase their status, and the position of alpha is always under threat. This is an expected part of our way of life, and it certainly isn't unacceptable for us. My sister may be extremely ambitious, but that isn't wrong in the eyes of a wolftaur. Murder is though, but the only one that could be directly linked with that was me. So I bore the brunt of it until I couldn't do so any more. I also did not want my father to suffer the consequences either, so I asked him to expel me from the pack."

"What? You mean you can never go back?"

"No. It was not complete banishment. In fact I have been back recently in an effort to regain my place in the pack. I'll be going back again soon to pursue that goal. However, by expelling me, Chrisen, my father, reconsolidated his position. He had managed to hang onto the position of alpha despite what had happened because he's an unusually strong person, both mentally and physically, but this move stabilised the whole pack by bringing some sort of acceptable resolution to the crisis."

"I see. And how did you end up with Goldfur?"

Lupu looked a little embarrassed. "As I said, I wasn't much into hunting. In fact, after I was expelled, I came close to starving because I wasn't skilled at it. I did have one stroke of fortune though. At the time, my pack was camped not too far away from the village of the Mountain Glade foxtaur clan. When I stumbled upon their community, I was too proud to ask for food though, so I took to raiding for it. The foxtaurs don't lock their doors, so I had ready access to their kitchens and pantries."

"So, rather than beg for food, you became a thief? How did that satisfy your pride?"

Lupu looked genuinely ashamed now. "It's easier to justify yourself when you don't have to come face to face with anybody. Anyway, it turns out that I wasn't too good at that either however. I made too much noise, and was caught one evening when someone heard me and came out to investigate. That someone was Goldfur. I might have gotten away if I hadn't been so surprised by seeing a chakat for the first time. I certainly didn't know their capabilities, especially that prehensile tail. After shi lassoed my legs as I tried to dash past hir and I fell flat on my face, shi waited for me to calm down and invited me to dinner. Ha! I still can't believe it. Just like that, shi took me in. Now I realise that it was hir empathic sense that told hir much about me, as well as my skin and bones physique, but then I was left wondering why anyone would take a thief into their family. Shi didn't even tell hir foxtaur relatives that I had been stealing food, only that I was a friend in need whom shi had invited over for a meal. I stuffed myself until I was nearly ill, and even then Goldfur saw to it that I had somewhere to sleep it off."

"That sure sounds like something shi'd do, considering what shi did for me. Shi didn't hesitate a moment to try helping me out either. I knew the chakats tend to be sociable and helpful, but it seems that goes deeper than I originally realised. Must have come as a bit of a shock to you though, having no experience with them before."

"You got that right! If someone had come raiding my pack's supplies, they might have been ripped apart! Instead, she fed me and gave me shelter. Heh! Shi even made me take a bath, and saw to it personally. That's also when I learned that shi's a hermaphrodite, a concept that I hadn't even heard of before, but I was immediately fascinated. Shi contained all the qualities of both my father and my mother rolled into one. I found this extremely attractive and I wanted to stick around to learn more. Goldfur offered me a deal. If I would take on cub-minding and other duties to free up hir time, I could stay on with hir family. I don't think either of us counted on me falling in love with hir."

"I find it surprising that you fell in love so quickly. You sure that it wasn't just a case of hero-worship?" Dale asked thoughtfully.

"I wasn't sure either when I offered Goldfur a cub in gratitude, but I don't regret that decision. We weren't sure that I'd get pregnant though, but it turns out that many taurs have some degree of compatibility. However, shi wouldn't accept without formalising the relationship. Unlike the wolftaur pack where the alphas have full breeding privileges with any other member of the pack, chakats won't have children with anyone unless they are a declared mate, even when they are the alpha of their family like Goldfur is. It startled me when shi asked me to become hir denmate, but I happily accepted. I proudly bore hir twins."

Dale frowned in puzzlement. "Twins? I don't recall seeing a second besides Stonefur."

Lupu looked infinitely sad for a moment before she shook herself and turned the memory away. "Greypaw was killed in the *Humans First* riot last year."

"Oh! I'm so sorry, Lupu!"

"It's okay, Dale. I'll always miss my cub, but I've mostly put that behind me now."

"Does it give you any problems that I am... *was* a human?"

"No, dear. I have some very good human friends, and I certainly don't blame all humans for the acts of some bigoted fools. Anyway, you've been hurt by those same people."

"Huh? How do you mean?"

Lupu looked surprised for a moment, then the realisation dawned. "Oh! You never heard the news. The *Humans First* movement has been blamed for the sabotage of the transporter. The Star Corps is one of the biggest targets for these terrorists due to the large number of morphs employed by them."

Conflicting emotions consumed Dale. He felt rage because this had been a deliberate act of sabotage that had resulted in his plight, but also shame that it had been his own kind that had perpetrated this heinous act. Then there was the irony that the only one that they had managed to directly harm was a fellow human! Dale trembled for several seconds while Lupu watched him with concern, then he visibly deflated. All his anger and humiliation helped him not one bit, and so he tried his best to calm himself. Eventually he regained control, and he turned to Lupu and said, "Thank you for telling me this, Lupu."

Lupu nodded. "Now that you've heard my story, perhaps you can tell me more about you?"

Dale was glad to get his mind off the latest revelation. "I suppose that's only fair, but I really don't know what I could tell you. My life was dead boring in comparison. I mean, that's why I left the farm life in the first place, because it was so dull. Maybe you'd like to hear more about my travels?" he asked hopefully.

Lupu was going to ask him instead for more details about what he and Mary-Anne found interesting to do together, when Forestwalker walked into the room.

"Ah! There you are! I just wanted to warn you that a couple of Star Corps specialists are going to be arriving soon. We called them earlier this morning to tell them that you were sleeping soundly and we didn't want to disturb you, so they deferred their visit until a little later. However, they couldn't let it go too long or they wouldn't make it today, so they're actually due any moment."

"Thanks, Forest. I should have remembered that they were going to send some people to see me. Umm, there's one other thing that you could help me with…"

Forestwalker immediately realised what he meant. "Okay. Do you want to attend to it now?"

Dale nodded, getting up onto all four paws. He turned to Lupu and said, "Thanks for the talk, Lupu. You've helped me a lot, believe me."

"You're welcome, Dale," she replied with a smile.

Dale then left with Forestwalker, declining the offer of support, preferring instead to practice walking on his own. They made their way to the bathroom where Forestwalker helped him out again.

While he had been assuaging his hunger and talking with Lupu, the household had been going about its normal activities. Trina could be found hard at work on one of her architectural projects. Goldfur had been going over the details of hir work on the space station with Midnight, who in turn had been apprising hir of upcoming Star Corps and Star Fleet projects which could be of interest to hir and Garrek. Forestwalker had been splitting hir time between all the various cubs and doing household chores, many of which had been left waiting for quite some time while the chakat sisters had been busy with their careers. In other words, everyone was doing normal, everyday things in an effort to cope with the current extraordinary events. However, Goldfur knew that Dale's situation would probably get worse before his steps forward exceeded his setbacks. When he wandered into the study where shi and Midnight were talking, shi knew that it was time to let him know about the latest news in regards to the visiting Star Corps specialists.

"You seem to be walking a little better this morning, Dale," shi started off conversationally.

"A little," he agreed. "An odd half-dream this morning seemed to... well... put me more in touch with this body." He promptly stumbled over his own tail, showing that his gain had been minor indeed. He grunted in annoyance and plonked down heavily on his rump.

Goldfur winced a little, then sighed to hirself. "I'm glad that you woke up when you did. Forest told you about the specialists who are coming to see you?"

"Yeah. So who am I to expect?" Dale asked.

"The psych evaluator that you have an appointment with

is coming first. Then some medical specialists."

Dale grimaced. "Sounds like fun," he said sarcastically.

Goldfur couldn't think of anything to say to that, so shi continued on with hir news. "I did get a call from a physical therapist who heard about your situation. A skunktaur called Queznal has been working on a radical new technique and wants to try it out on you."

"So I'm to be guinea pig now too?" Dale said acerbically.

"Don't take it like that, Dale. I checked into hys background and found out that hy has been doing some groundbreaking work in physical therapy. I reckon that you could do a *lot* worse than to see if hy can help you help you with this new technique."

Dale's ire deflated and he sighed. "Okay. I don't suppose I really have much choice anyway, and if I'm going to be stuck in this body, then I'd like to get it up to speed as soon as possible." Then another thought crossed his mind. "*Hy*? *Hys*? What sort of words are those?"

"Don't you know anything about skunktaurs?" Midnight asked. "Goldfur and I have worked with them a number of times on various Star Corps projects."

Dale shook his head. "I suppose my line of work didn't bring me into contact with them. I've heard about them, but haven't really learned much about them. I thought they all lived on Chakona?"

"Most do nowadays," Midnight answered, "But there are still some to be found on Earth. Their kind doesn't exactly have a love for humans, considering their history. The ones that do live or work on this planet are usually the more forgiving or open-minded ones. Anyway, that doesn't answer your question. The words "hys" and "hy" are the pronouns created for the skunktaurs. You see, they're a dual sex race also."

"They're herms like the chakats? Why don't they use the same pronouns as them then?"

"Well, they're not exactly like us," Goldfur said. "While we're both sexes at the same time, skunktaurs shift sexes mostly at will, so they're either male or female, but not both simultaneously. So people came up with a new set of pronouns to match their unique situation. It drives people crazy in languages where they don't have that flexibility though!" shi added with a grin.

Dale was about to make another comment but the door chime rang just then. Midnight jumped up and started trotting to the door, saying, "I'll get it. It's probably our expected visitors." Moments later, shi led two humans into the room, one male, one female. Steering them to Dale, shi introduced them. "Dale, these are Dr Gladstone, the psych evaluator, and Dr Kirrawong, a med tech expert."

Dale held out a hand to shake that of the others. As he did so, Dale looked them over. Gladstone stood a little taller than Dale's new height, about five feet ten inches tall he estimated. Dale noted his short, brown, neatly cut hair, soft features, and hazel eyes that regarded him warmly without seeming to stare. He dressed neatly in a sports jacket and Dale was amused to see that his tie had Ludwig von Drake upon it. He guessed that Gladstone carefully cultivated this comforting air for the benefit of his patients. Kirrawong gave a strikingly different impression. Judging by her broad, dark features and hair, she was quite obviously of Australian aboriginal descent. She dressed neatly but rather casually. Dale had heard of her and knew that she was a well-respected leader in her profession, so he presumed that she did not much care if people judged her by her looks because her achievements spoke for themselves.

"Pleased to meet you, I think," Dale said. "I thought that just the psych evaluator was coming first?"

Kirrawong smiled. "He's a little bit late and I'm a little bit early, but we'd both like to see you together for a couple of minutes, if that's okay with you?"

Dale shrugged. "It's not as if I have anything better to do. Do what you need to do. Just tell me that any of it's going to be of any use."

Gladstone spoke up in a calm and reassuring voice. "You know already that we will be trying everything possible, and it certainly hasn't come to the point of no hope. It's important that you keep this in mind."

"Yeah, yeah," Dale agreed cynically. "Let's just get this over and done with, hey?"

"Certainly," Gladstone nodded. He turned to Goldfur. "Shir Goldfur, is there are room we may borrow for the examination?"

Shi nodded. "This way," shi said as shi started padding off in the direction of a room that wasn't presently being used. Opening the door shi ushered them inside. "Just call if you want anything."

Kirrawong patted the sophisticated sensor unit slung over her shoulder. "I've got everything that I need right here, thank you."

The three were together in the room for about ten minutes before Kirrawong came out again. Goldfur and Midnight looked up from the paperwork on the table in mild surprise. "Done so soon, doctor?" Midnight inquired.

She smiled reassuringly. "Yes. I was mostly after some readings to check whether anything that we brainstormed last night would be of any use, and to check whether his condition was stable. The good news is that he seems to be a normal healthy chakat. The bad news is that not one of our ideas is worth a pinch of bulldust, so it's back to the drawing board."

"I thought as much," Goldfur said. "I'm familiar with transporter equipment, but I couldn't think of anything to undo this without Dale's original pattern."

Kirrawong lost her smile for a moment as she nodded in agreement. "We tend to agree, but it wouldn't be fair to Mr. Perkins to not try."

"So we'd best concentrate on getting him to accept his new form?"

"Well, there's always the chance of giving him a new human form. Even if it's not his original one, he may find that preferable to being stuck in a totally different and uncomfortable form, no offence meant."

"None taken," Goldfur replied. "I understand what you mean. As fond as I am of my bipedal friends and family, I certainly don't want to be one."

Kirrawong's smile returned. "Then I'd better get back to the lab and see what we can do. A pleasure meeting you two."

Goldfur saw to Kirrawong's departure, but it was quite a while before they could do the same for Gladstone. A couple of hours passed before he and Dale emerged from the room. Gladstone looked exactly as he had when he went in, but Dale looked very tired. Goldfur tried to gauge his state with hir empathic senses. Shi detected a calmness about him that hadn't been there previously which gave hir much relief. Evidently, while the interview had been tiring, the effort had been worth it. He shook hands with Gladstone before excusing himself and heading off to his room. When he was out of earshot, Goldfur asked, "So how is shi? We've been concerned about how shi's been coping with all this."

"Without violating confidentiality between me and my

patient, I can tell you that Mr. Perkins is a young and tough. I think he'll cope, but it's up to all of us to see that he makes the best of his circumstances as possible. Right now, his self-image is severely shaken and the less anyone does to affect the fragile new balance, the better. Your question is a perfect example. You refer to Mr. Perkins as *shi* and *hir*, but he does not see himself as a hermaphrodite despite his new body. We are all more than our gender, but an important part of it is wrapped up in that and he still pictures himself as a male. I would get into the habit of thinking and speaking of him as a male in future. It's a small thing, but one that might have rather great repercussions at this stage."

Goldfur nodded slowly, thinking of the problems ahead. "That sounds fair enough, but what happens when hir... umm... his body does utterly female things? He has already been subjected to lactating, and he will soon be coming into heat. Male self-image isn't going to stop *that*."

"I agree, but there may be ways of ameliorating the effects. Is there someone female, not a herm, who may be close to him?"

Goldfur gave him a sour look. "Not that we know of. He had a girlfriend whom we had hoped might be of assistance, but almost as soon as she heard about what had happened to him, she disassociated herself from any further relationship with Dale." Goldfur's expression told volumes about what she thought of a person who would do this to someone with whom she was supposedly intimately involved. "We don't know of anyone else…" Shi was interrupted by Midnight touching hir on the arm to get hir attention.

"What about Lupu?" Midnight asked. "She seems to like him, and she's all female. I think Dale likes her too after he got over their initial troubles."

Goldfur blinked, then slowly nodded. "You may be right." Turning back to Gladstone, shi said, "Lupu's a wolftaur bitch who's my denmate. Does it matter that she's not human?"

Gladstone replied, "While the human former girlfriend would have been better, any kind of female will do if there's at least something they share between them. I would observe them closely, use that empathic talent of yours and try to judge whether their association is helping Dale. If Lupu can see him as a male and treat him that way, it would bolster his battered ego a lot. And by the way, don't forget that he now also has the physical equipment to sense things empathically, only he hasn't had the upbringing and training on how to use it. At the moment it's mostly a wide open door and *everything* just pours in. Dale brought up the embarrassing first encounter with Lupu, although he didn't give me much background on her. He was just detailing the difficulties he had been having at the time. It's obvious now that Lupu, a non-empath with no training to control her emotional output, virtually buried him in a flood of affection and sheer sexual desire. He had no way of shutting it off, nor controlling it. It's hardly any wonder that he reacted so strongly to her. I wouldn't be surprised if some sort of bond might have occurred as a result of that inadvertent intimacy."

A light dawned on Goldfur. "Would this have been going both ways?" shi asked.

"Quite possibly. Chakats project as well as receive."

Goldfur looked at Midnight who nodded, knowing what shi was thinking. Shi turned back to the psych tech. "That would explain why Lupu has been acting the way she has lately. Shi's been having her own difficulties too, and has been showing some dissatisfaction with her current circumstances. Now suddenly she's become as excited as a puppy whenever Dale is mentioned. I think she's formed an empathic bond with Dale. Many know about our empathic gifts, but few realise how far-reaching they can be. When we have very strong feelings for someone, we sometimes form this bond, and once it has come into existence, it never breaks. I have such a bond with my lifemates, and especially my sister, Forestwalker. I can still sense hir even when I'm far off in space somewhere. Now Dale and Lupu might both be sensing each other's emotions without even realising it."

"You could be right. I'd hesitate to confirm it without a much longer period of observation, but if you're right, Lupu could indeed be the best thing for him right now, and possibly for her too. Are *you* going to have a problem with this? She is *your* denmate after all."

"Lupu has always been free to do whatever she decides is best for her. I care for Lupu a lot, but she isn't a soulmate like my beloved first lifemate. It remains Lupu's choice. I won't try to influence her either way."

"Fine. Continue letting them associate as much as possible and monitor Mr. Perkins's responses. Be as discreet and understanding as possible when dealing with unavoidable female issues, although I dare say I don't really need to tell you that. I'll be in regular contact to monitor his progress, and don't hesitate to call me in the event of a crisis."

"Thank you, Mr. Gladstone," Goldfur said, shaking his hand and starting to lead him to the front door. "I'll admit that psychology isn't my strong suit, so I'll be most grateful for your assistance when necessary."

"You're welcome, Shir Goldfur. I must admit that this will be of great personal interest, so it's not a great disruption to my usual routine," he added with a quiet smile, the first Goldfur had seen on him.

Goldfur smiled back as shi opened the door and let the doctor out. Shi met Midnight coming back from the direction of Dale's room who reported that shi had found their guest sprawled out on the bedding, fast asleep.

"I reckon that he was pretty much exhausted by that session," Midnight said. "How long before this Queznal person turns up?"

"Hy said hy would be able to come out early this evening, if that wasn't inconvenient."

"Fine by me. We can get some work done on *our* projects in the meantime. I mean, they might be still paying you to keep an eye on our guest, but that doesn't get any of your work done, nor are they paying *me* for that time. If we're going to be able to afford a new den that's big enough for both our families, we need to turn in these projects on time."

Goldfur nodded mutely in agreement. Midnight had the more practical mind of the two, and Goldfur valued hir dedication to the job at hand, especially when shi got hirself into situations like this current one. Shi had gone back to work so soon after giving birth to Tailstalker because of their need for as much income as possible. They were paid well but a new home that was big enough for a horde of chakats and other morphs would not be cheap, even splitting the costs with hir sister's family. However, it was obvious to all that the need to re-unite their families increased with every new cub. They had always been happiest when sharing this place, but the growth of their families had forced them to split up. The biggest problem with that though was that they no longer had as ready access to a cubsitter as they used to. Lupu had been a marvellous help, even after she had added her own cubs to the family, but she wouldn't always be available. It was worse for Forestwalker though. While Trina liked to play with the cubs, she too was a career person and they were proving to be too disruptive. Her seemingly inexhaustible energy was being stretched to the limit, and Forestwalker knew that it was unfair to impose more duties on her, despite the fact that one of the cubs was her own. The best and most popular solution was to merge their families again which would enable them to spread the cub-minding duties more effectively. However, they were all still young and, despite their well-paid jobs, not yet quite able to invest in a very large place without a bit of financial strain. Therefore, they all had to concentrate as best they could on their projects whenever they got the opportunity.

It was about six o'clock when a slightly bleary-eyed Dale stumbled into their office. "Umm, sorry about just disappearing like that. That session with Gladstone was rather tiring."

"No need to apologise, Dale. Would you like something to eat?" Goldfur asked. "Lupu's been cooking up a nice stew."

Dale's ears perked up at the sound of that, although Goldfur wasn't sure whether it was the mention of food or the wolftaur that prompted that response. "I'll check it out, I think," he said with a smile. Goldfur watched him go with a small grin on hir muzzle.

* * *

"Hi Lupu," Dale greeted the wolftaur.

She looked up from the pot that she was stirring, her face lighting up in pleasure. "Dale! How are you feeling? Would you like some stew? I make it to a wolftaur recipe and this hungry horde seems to like it."

"I'd love some!" he replied fervently.

""Then just park your butt over by the table and I'll serve you up a dollop." She put action to words and ladled out a generous portion, padding over to the table to place it under Dale's muzzle. The intensity of the smell startled him until he realised that his new senses were far keener. He'd already started drooling in anticipation as he grabbed a fork to start eating. A little self-consciously, he licked the drool from his lips before taking a mouthful. The taste practically exploded on his tongue. It was magnificent!

Lupu was watching his reactions and smiled when she saw his face light up. "It's all in the herbs. They really bring out the flavours."

Dale mumbled a nearly incomprehensible agreement as he

started shovelling the food in. He was hungry, but adding the delicious taste, he became nearly ravenous. Lupu grinned in satisfaction with his reaction. It didn't take him long to finish off his serving. He looked at the empty plate, wondering if he should ask for more.

"Leave some for the others," Lupu laughed. "If there's any left over, I'll give you seconds."

"Thanks, Lupu," Dale said, handing the large plate back to her. "I hope you make this again soon."

Taking the plate to the sink, Lupu replied, "What? You don't want to try my other recipes? I know a few more culinary tricks, you know?"

"Oh no! I mean, of course I want to try your other recipes..." He came to a stop as he realised that Lupu was laughing.

"I'm just teasing you, dear. Of course I'll make this again if you'd really like it. It's one of my favourites too, as a matter of fact." She trotted back over and put her hand on his arm, suddenly semi-serious again. "So how are you feeling now, Dale?"

"Better for the food, and the talk with the psych evaluator. At least a little more optimistic. Now if only I can get this body to work for me the way I want it to, then things'll be even better."

Lupu gave him a hug. "Patience, Dale. I think you're already doing a *lot* better than you were yesterday when I met you. I think you'll do fine." She paused, looking at him for a moment, a little bit puzzled why she felt so strongly about him, then shrugged mentally. She liked him, and that was all that mattered. The fact that he resembled her denmate helped, but it was his different attitude that she found refreshing. She decided she wanted to spend a bit more time with him. Just then, Goldfur came into the dining area with Forestwalker. Shi had just arrived home from an outing with hir cubs and was a little tired. Shi licked hir lips with anticipation as shi smelled the delicious aroma of the stew.

"Is dinner ready, Lupu?" Forest asked hopefully.

"Sure is! Go unbury Trina from her computer and I'll have the meal served by the time you get back."

"Will do! Back in a jiffy!" Forest bounded off in the direction of Trina's office. Midnight arrived first though, but it took surprisingly little time for Forest to retrieve hir lifemate, although the smell of the stew permeating the house probably had something to do with hir alacrity. The cubs were served first, then the adults sat down to enjoy their meal. Kris turned up when they were about halfway through, slightly miffed at them not waiting for him.

"You don't really think that you can hold up this bunch of hungry chakats, do you, love?" Trina inquired after giving him a greeting cuddle.

"No, but I'd like to get home for once before I have to scrape the pan for the dregs!" Kris replied wistfully.

Lupu plonked a full plate in front of him. "Oh, cut the theatrics and dig in!"

Kris looked up at her with a grateful grin. "Thanks, Lupu. I knew you wouldn't let me starve." This statement caused him to be bombarded with napkins from the rest of the family, laughing at his antics.

*   *   *

Queznal turned up about 7:30pm. Hy was a typical skunktaur, similar in size, although not in weight, to a chakat. Hys build was lighter, but otherwise similar to a chakat's, right down to the digitigrade hind feet. Anyone who was familiar with natural skunks would know that they're plantigrade, but the geneticists who created the skunktaur race had basically stolen the base coding from the progenitors of the chakat race, so they stuck with the digitigrade feet. They had not retained the chakats' forepaws however, and they had normal feet instead of their chakat kin's handpaws. The most striking difference however was their fur. While their patterning might vary, they all had the deep black, long fur with white markings that were distinctive to skunks. The tail was huge and bushy and quite attractive. Queznal's was no different, and hy sported a spotted patterning with only modest striping on hys tail. One other feature that set the skunktaurs apart was the paw shaped mark on their right breast. It came in only three colours: black, red and blue, denoting not only clan, but also hys particular Talent. Queznal had a red paw mark, denoting that he was a telepath. This could be clearly seen as he wore no clothes except for a light open vest that was evidently just for show. Hy had a belt around his waist in which he housed such things as a lightweight tricorder and hys personal effects.

Queznal was in male phase at this time, something that Goldfur felt could only be of benefit when dealing with Dale and his problem. Shi idly wondered if hy had shifted sexes specifically for the occasion. Skunktaurs very frequently preferred their male phase, which had led them to being referred to as the chakats' brothers, but that didn't mean that was the case with Queznal. It took some time to accomplish the change, which might explain why hy had put off the encounter until this evening. Chakats had always considered skunktaurs their brethren and shi greeted hym in the manner in which shi usually greeted a new chakat – a brief but heartfelt hug and a full introduction. "I am Chakat Goldfur, child of Longstripe and Desertsand."

"A pleasure to meet you, Longstripe's daughter. I am Queznal of House Redpaw, child of Marky and Vannen."

"Come in and make yourself at home, Queznal," Goldfur said with a smile. "Can I get you anything?"

"Thanks. I'd like to get straight to work if I can, although I could do with a cuppa tea if possible," hy replied hopefully.

"No problem. I'll get you one in a moment." They walked into the living room where Dale was lounging on the floor, talking with Midnight, exchanging tales of what each had done on various planets. "First I'll introduce you to your patient. Dale, this is Doctor Queznal."

Dale got up to all fours with only trifling unsteadiness and held out his hand. Queznal shook it solemnly, not offering a hug because hy realised that hy was dealing with someone who was a chakat in body only. The two exchanged pleasantries until Goldfur returned with a large mug of tea.

"Help yourself to milk or sugar," shi said, indicating the jug and bowl on the coffee table.

"Thanks, Goldfur," Queznal said appreciatively, pouring only a little milk but spooning three lots of sugar into the mug. Hy took a long swig and aahed in pleasure. "I needed that." Hy then put the mug down and switched moods slightly. "Right, let's get this under way. Basically, I'm developing a radical new means of dealing with paraplegics. Despite our ability to repair a lot of nerve damage, we still have problems rehabilitating the patients due to the complexity of the nervous system, especially the spinal cord. You, Dale, are the perfect subject for a test run because you possess a perfectly healthy chakat body, although one that you don't properly control. I believe that I can get you doing everything just like a normal chakat in a very short time, especially as Goldfur is here to help."

"Me?" said Goldfur, startled. "How can *I* help?"

"I need your empathic ability a bit, but mainly because you're Dale's identical twin, so there are no unknowns to spoil the results. You are going to supply the correct feedback for Dale so that he will know how to do something without having to think about it."

"And how am I supposed to do that?" shi asked.

"That's the essence of my new treatment." Queznal paused to finish drinking hys tea and put the mug down on the table. Hy gestured to the red-coloured fur on hys chest. "As you should be able to tell by my clan mark, I am a telepath. My Talent rating is T6."

This impressed Goldfur a lot, but Dale was forced to ask, "What exactly does that entail?"

"It means that I have abilities over and beyond those of most telepathic skunktaurs. Not only is my ability stronger than usual, but I have subtle talents that almost no others do. I'm trying to put those abilities to use in my profession. To make a long story short, I plan to link you and Goldfur to provide physical and mental feedback. You are going to learn which muscles do what directly from the owner of the original template!"

"You're going to read my mind? Dale asked uncertainly.

"No. That is unethical and I would never do that without your permission. I'm just going to act as a conduit between you two and I'll be instructing you how to use this link."

Goldfur spoke up. "Perhaps it would be best if we get straight into it and you can explain as we go?"

"I was about to suggest the same," hy replied with a smile. "Do you want to do it here, or is there a more suitable place?"

"We'll use the room that the others used when checking Dale," Goldfur replied, getting up to lead the way. Shi ushered in the other two then closed the door behind them.

"Good, this will do perfectly," Queznal said. "Now, would the two of you please stand on either side of me, facing in the same direction as I am."

They complied, and the three of them were quickly lined up in a short row. Queznal took out hys tricorder and switched it to voice recording mode. Hy spoke loudly and clearly, "I am about to initiate a telepathic link between myself, Dale Perkins and Chakat Goldfur for the purposes of a new type of physical therapy that I am developing utilising telepathic gestalt. Do you, Dale, consent to this procedure?"

Dale nodded slowly, then said, "I guess so. Anything that will help me to get about in this body better will be a bonus."

"And you, Goldfur, do you also consent?"

Goldfur said without hesitation, "I do."

Queznal switched modes on the tricorder to monitor the work hy was about to do. "Okay, that takes care of the formalities for the ethics committee. Let's get some real work done." Hy lifted hys arms and put a hand lightly on their heads. "I am about to initiate a link between your minds, with myself as the conduit and controller. Goldfur, you shouldn't feel anything. I'll just be using you as a data source essentially. Just follow any instructions that I give you, please. Dale, I am going to ask Goldfur to make a series of movements which I'm going to have you try to imitate. While you try, I will feed you the same neural impulses that Goldfur creates to make the muscles move in the desired manner. What I hope to achieve is for your mind to associate those impulses with the appropriate movement. Please don't be concerned if you feel yourself doing something that you don't expect because this will only be the result of the feedback that I will be channelling to you. Are you ready?"

"Just get on with it," Dale replied a little irritably. Goldfur just nodded.

"Okay. Goldfur, please lift your right forepaw until it's about twenty centimetres off the floor, then put it down again. Dale, you try to do the same." Goldfur did so, Dale jerkily imitating. "No, you're resisting me. Here, let me show how it should go."

Dale's forepaw quickly lifted up into position and then down again.

"Whoa!" Dale exclaimed. "That felt weird. You were in complete control of my leg for a moment there, weren't you?"

"Yes, I was. However, that's not what I want to achieve. I want you to feel what Goldfur is doing *through* me, not me imposing it on you. Let's try again."

And so they did, several times, until Queznal was satisfied, then hy switched legs and started again. Then they worked on the hind legs, getting Goldfur to move them in various ways. Dale started getting the hang of the procedure and responding to the prompts first time. Without realising it, he opened up fully to Queznal who could then fully "teach" his mind to link actions with certain parts of his brain. The session went on for hours until such time as all the participants were feeling close to exhausted. By this time, virtually every muscle in Dale's lower anatomy had been prodded into action. Queznal broke the connection and Dale sank gratefully to the floor to rest. Queznal moved a little apart before hy too sat down on a lounging rug. Goldfur, who had the least to do, offered to fetch some refreshments for all, to which they both gratefully nodded. Shi brought back a jug of orange juice and some cake and they all quietly sated their thirst and hunger.

Eventually, Queznal broke the silence. "How are you feeling now, Dale?"

"Tired, but a good kind of tired. I can really feel those muscles now, and know what they do." He held up a handpaw and put his tail tip into it. "It's both weird and wonderful." He released his tail then got up and walked around the room without a stumble. Perhaps it wasn't as graceful as Goldfur would have done, but a stranger would have been hard pressed to pick a problem. He stopped in front of the skunktaur and said with great sincerity, "Thank you, Queznal. I don't know if I could have coped too much longer without your help."

Queznal smiled back, enormously satisfied with hys efforts. "No, thank you, Mr Perkins. You've provided me with a lot of data for my research. I'm only too glad to have been of help. If you wish, I can come back for a couple more sessions so that we can fine-tune your control."

"I'd like that. I can't tell you how much better I feel now that I'm more in control of my body again." Just then, the consequences of a long period without break plus a big drink started impinging on Dale's consciousness. He was about to ask to be excused when he remembered something. Then another thought crossed his mind and Goldfur clearly felt a wave of embarrassment come from him as he started asking Queznal a question. "Ummm, could I ask you one favour though?"

Although Queznal wasn't empathic like Goldfur, hy did note the telltale flush of pink inside Dale's ears and realised something was bothering him. "Go ahead, Dale. What is it?"

"Well, there's one group of muscles that we didn't try out, one that I really need to know…" He stopped, beginning to feel truly foolish.

Goldfur suddenly guessed what he was trying to say. Forest had told hir about Dale's problem last night and shi realised that gaining control over this function was just as important to him as the ability to walk straight, maybe even more. Shi decided that being blunt about it was the best approach. "I think he's talking about being able to control his penis to urinate properly."

Dale wanted to sink into the floor from embarrassment, but nodded in agreement. Queznal was sympathetic though. Hy said, "Dale, I quite understand. My work brings me into contact with paraplegics and quadriplegics all the time, and simple little things like that are of huge importance to them too. My work is intended not only to repair their bodies, but to restore their independence and pride also. I can see how this would be of importance to you and I'm certainly the one to ask. If you feel up to it, I'm prepared to give you one last quick session to help you in this."

"Thank you. I can handle it. I *want* to get this out of the way as soon as possible."

"Then assume the same positions again and we'll get it over in a jiffy," Queznal smiled.

They did so, and soon Dale was hoping that no one would walk in at that time. Both chakats felt extremely silly practicing extruding their penises, and even the normally clinically-detached skunktaur wasn't unaffected by the bizarre scene. Fortunately it didn't take too long. Dale was highly motivated and quickly got the hang of it. Queznal finished the session gratefully, hys Talent having been worked hard this evening. Hy prepared to depart.

"I'll be in contact with you soon, Dale. I want to follow up on this session and see how you're doing. If necessary, we can have another if there are any problems. Right now, I suggest getting as much practice as possible with what we have covered already, but don't be afraid to experiment. You've actually responded better than I had expected, and I can only hope that bodes well for my other patients too. However, unlike you, they have physical damage that needs to be overcome also, but that's why this work with you was so important. Everything I learn from you will be put into my research into helping these people."

"Then I'm glad my misfortune might help others. Thanks again, Doctor," Dale said.

"Just Queznal, please," hy said with a smile. "You're very welcome. However, now I must go. Here are my details if you need to contact me." Hy handed a smart card to Dale, then turned for the door. Goldfur opened it for hym and accompanied hym to the front door. "Thank you for your hospitality, Shir Goldfur. It's been a pleasure meeting you. Give my regards to your lifemate, Garrek."

"I'll do that, Queznal. Thanks again!" Goldfur replied and closed the door behind hym. Moments later shi realised that shi had never even mentioned Garrek while hy had been there.

* * *

Dale wasted no time in taking advantage of his newly acquired ability to go to the toilet by himself. He decided he'd never again take for granted such a simple thing as being able to have privacy in such circumstances. After that, he again had to milk himself. "This could get old real fast," he thought to himself. After taking the milk to the kitchen, he showed off his ability to walk about and keep his tail out of doors to Forestwalker, Midnight and especially Lupu. The latter gave him a congratulatory hug which made him feel even better.

"I have some good news, Dale," Lupu said after finishing the lengthy embrace.

"I could do with some, Lupu," he replied.

"We got a call from the Star Corps. They've managed to contact your parents on Mars at last. Took them long enough!"

Dale gave her a grimace. "They chose one of the more challenging frontiers. There's no subspace communications facilities out there. That means they'll have to make there way into one of the main settlements in order for us to have a conversation. That's one of the reasons I don't visit as often as I'd like. It's just too difficult getting there. Anyway, did they give you a time?"

Lupu nodded. "They've scheduled a contact for you at ten o'clock tomorrow morning. They told me tell you that they've been fully briefed on the accident, so you won't have to try to explain that."

Dale felt relieved. He hadn't been relishing the prospect of trying to explain to his parents that their son was now not even human. Of course, he had no idea how they were reacting to that news already, nor what path the conversation would take. He needed to talk to them though, so he prayed that this conversation would be better than the last he had on a comm.

Dale wanted to stay and chat with Lupu a bit longer, but a jaw-cracking yawn reminded him how tired he was after that session. Lupu chased him off to his bedroom, insisting that he get right to sleep, then ended up staying with him there for over an hour just talking. They told each other more about their families and friends that they hadn't shared before, and their hopes for the future. For the first time since the accident, Dale wasn't bitter about that and started looking at things a tad more optimistically. He found he enjoyed talking to the wolftaur. It helped that she was young, vivacious and, yes, quite sexy. However, tiredness soon overcame even this and Lupu decided to let him sleep, but not before she gave him a long cuddle and a lick-kiss goodnight. Dale found himself grinning in pleasure as he settled down to sleep.

* * *

Dale abruptly woke up early, his hearts pumping, his body tense, screaming out a need for something that he didn't understand. He got to his feet and opened the door, intending to head for the bathroom to try to splash himself with water, or anything that might help, only to encounter Midnight passing through. Shi gave him a cheery "*Good Morning*" and headed for the kitchen. Dale got a whiff of hir scent and the feeling of desire exploded within him. Although he didn't realise it, he could smell hir pheromones, and shi was in male phase. To his horror, he was feeling an intense sexual desire for hir, and it was *not* as a male. Involuntarily, a howl of mixed anguish, confusion and frustration broke from his throat. Within moments, several of the inhabitants of the house were at his side, but that only served to make things worse. Goldfur knew immediately what the problem was though and, after a quick word to Forestwalker, shi immediately shooed off everybody else and guided Dale back to his room.

"Just lie down to try to relax, Dale. Forest will be back in a moment with something that will help you," shi started saying.

"What's happening to me?" Dale interrupted. "I feel like so strange. Part of me aches for something. God help me, I smelled Midnight and all I could think of was I wanted hir to mount me!" Dale's voice was climbing into hysteria.

"Calm down, Dale. You've gone into heat, that's all. Forest is bringing a herbal drink that will lessen the effects."

"Into *heat*? That's *all*? How can I be in heat? I'm a heterosexual male! I can't be in heat and wanting to be mounted. I just *can't*!"

Goldfur realised that he wasn't thinking clearly and was reacting badly to this new development. Shi put hir arms around him and tried using hir empathic gifts to soothe him, but such was the depth of his feelings that shi had very little effect. Shi sighed in relief when Forestwalker arrived with a mug of what looked like herbal tea. Shi took it from hir, then tried to get Dale to drink the contents.

"You must drink this, Dale. It's a very strong suppressant. It's about the only thing that works on chakats because of our immunity to most poisons and drugs. It *will* help you though."

Dale finally got it through his hormone-soaked thoughts that this would alleviate his problems and he almost frantically snatched the mug from Goldfur and drained the contents virtually in one gulp. Although the effects weren't instantaneous, the herbal mix did work quickly and it wasn't long before the rampant physical effects were brought down to a bearable level. Both Goldfur and Forestwalker worked on empathically calming him all the while until he was ready to talk again.

Forest said, "Tell us what happened when you woke up, Dale. Just take it easy and calmly."

Dale explained as best he could. When he mentioned

Midnight, both chakats cursed softly. He looked quizzically at them. Goldfur started explaining, "Midnight has just hit the height of male phase and hir scent is at its most potent. Shi was the worst possible person to meet this morning when you were vulnerable and didn't understand what was happening. One whiff of hir pheromones was more than enough to set you off."

"But if I'm on heat, that means you should be too. Why aren't you affected too?"

"I *am* affected. However, I've had the benefit of training and years of experience in dealing with it. All chakats learn about these things from an early age because they *need* to. Even so, the first time is the hardest. However, we'll do our best to help you through this."

"How?" Dale asked sceptically. "It's not as if I'm a real chakat and don't mind the thought of having sex that way."

"I know, it's not going to be easy," Forest said, "But we'll do what we can. Lie down and try to relax. Let the herbal drink do its work. We'll be back soon to try some things."

"For lack of any better ideas, Dale agreed and settled down. The sisters walked out of earshot and then Goldfur turned worriedly to hir sister.

"I don't like this, Forest. It's hitting him far harder than I expected. You felt his emotions? He was just about ready to charge through us to get to Midnight, and the realisation of this was tearing him up inside."

Forestwalker glumly nodded. "You're right, Goldie, but you said it yourself: the first time is always the hardest."

"But he's got my body, and it has *already* made the transition. It shouldn't be as bad as *this*!"

"You're forgetting something though. *First Heat* isn't just a matter of physical maturity for us. It's also the time when we make the mental transition from an academic point of view about sex to a genuine *need* for sexual intimacy. We knew what to expect, but not only doesn't Dale know that, he doesn't *want* to make that change. He's going to fight it all the way, only he can't win, and that's going to rip him apart psychologically."

"Oh, hell! I think you're right. I never thought about it as a First Heat situation. Maybe we should give Dr Gladstone a call…" Goldfur was interrupted by the sound of someone clearing their throat.

Lupu was standing in the doorway, apparently having been listening to the conversation. When she had the chakats' attention, she walked up to them and said, "Let me have a try."

Both sisters were a little surprised. Goldfur said, "We know you like Dale a lot, but what makes you think that you can help where we can't?"

Lupu's jaw dropped in a wolfish grin. "It's *because* you're herms and you just aren't used to thinking in single sex terms. Despite his body, Dale is a heterosexual male, and you keep thinking of his plight in herm terms. He's not one mentally though and what he wants is a female, even if his body is telling him otherwise. I reckon I know a way to satisfy both his needs."

Goldfur and Forestwalker looked at each other. At this close range, their empathic senses were clearly telling them that Lupu had an extra motive also. Not that it came as a surprise to them because they'd already figured out that Lupu and Dale had bonded. They gave each other a nod of agreement and Goldfur said to Lupu, "Okay, go for it! I'll hold off calling Gladstone for now, but if it doesn't work, let us know as soon as possible."

"Thanks! Just give me a moment to grab something and I'll get to work straight away." Lupu hurried off to her den, emerging moments later carrying a small box with her to Dale's room. Goldfur gave a start of recognition, then grinned and shook hir head, chuckling.

Forest noticed his sister's reaction and demanded, "Spit it out! What's so amusing?"

"Oh, just a little something that Lupu sometimes likes to try with me. Y'know, I think it just might work."

* * *

Lupu entered the room with a mixture of excitement and uncertainty. She was about to take a big step, both for herself and for Dale, and she hoped that she didn't muck it up. She still wasn't even sure why she was so overwhelmingly attracted to Dale, but she could literally feel his need and wanted to do her best to fulfil it. She saw that Dale was curled in on himself, apparently trying to get comfortable. "Dale? Are you awake?"

Dale rolled over and got up to his feet. Despite trying to relax, his body was far too keyed up to do so. Lupu's arrival though added to his excitement in one way, but calmed him down in another. He felt much better in her presence than he had with the chakats. "Hello, Lupu. I hadn't expected you. Ummm, I didn't disturb you with that racket that I made earlier, did I?"

"No, dear. I was already up. However, I do know about your problem and I'd like to help you if I can."

Now there was nothing better that Dale wanted to do than spend some time with this beautiful wolftaur bitch, but in his current condition, he didn't know how he'd feel or react, and so he hesitated a long time before answering. "Can you really help? Despite that drink they gave me, I still feel like crawling up the walls and doing something that I might regret."

Lupu put her hand on his cheek. "Do you trust me, Dale?" she asked.

Dale stared into hir dark eyes, feeling once again the

strange attraction to her that he didn't want to resist. "Yes, I think so. What are you going to do?"

"I'm going to soothe your physically desires, of course!" she said with a grin, then her expression became serious again. "I think I know what you are, Dale. From the moment we met, although I didn't know it at the time, I was attracted to your maleness. You're not like Goldfur; you project a different attitude, and it's one I like. Is there any doubt in your mind that I, a female, find you very attractive?"

Dale was a little surprised by the suddenness of this admission, and her candidness, but her words jibed with his own unspoken feelings for her. "No. No there isn't, and I'll say right now, although I don't understand why I have this overwhelming need for you, I feel the same way. But how's this going to help me with my problem?"

She patted the box she was holding. "Something in here is going to help with that. I just first wanted to establish how we stand together. I want you to know first that I'm thrilled to pieces that you like me as much as I like you." She paused to give him a hug and a quick lick-kiss. "Now, I asked you if you trusted me. I want to do something that will relieve you of the female cravings, but you must think of the process as you doing it to me."

Dale was completely puzzled. "I don't understand, Lupu."

"I know, I'm sorry. I just don't want to shock you. Let me show you and give me a chance to explain." She opened the box and pulled out the device within. There was a plastic-looking tubular object that was bent near the middle and tapered quickly at both ends. A leather harness was attached to it near the bend.

Dale quickly recognised what it was despite the odd shape. "Isn't that a sort of strap-on dildo?" he asked in concerned fascination.

"Yes, a very special one designed for taurs. I've used it

when Goldfur has been in female phase and in the mood. It's double-ended so that we both are pleasured at the same time. The harness is attached in such a way that as I thrust it into hir, it pivots on the connection and pushes more deeply into me at the same time. Dale, I want to use it on you."

"What? No! I keep telling people that I'm *not* a herm. I'm not a female either despite what's happening to me. I… I can't stand the thought of that *thing* being pushed inside of me."

"But you haven't heard what I intend to do yet. When I do use it, I want you to concentrate on how each thrust is actually going into me too, pleasuring me as only a male can. I want you to make love to me! Don't think of it as dildo, think of it as a fun way of coupling with me. I want you as a male to make love to me as a female, and at the same time we can relieve the needs of your new body. Will you do this for me, Dale? I want this so much!"

Lupu's arguments still hadn't convinced Dale. The idea of being penetrated even with this device was an alien thought to him. "I'm sorry Lupu, I just can't do it. Or at least, I can't do it yet."

Lupu felt as if he had given her a body blow. The proud wolftaur felt the stirring of anger within her because he had so readily rejected what she had offered. "Why won't you try?" she demanded. "Nobody else can do anything for you, and here I am offering *myself* to you and it's not good enough for you? In fact, everybody has been trying to help you and you keep responding by making things as hard as possible for them."

"What?! I *never* asked anyone to help me. If Goldfur hadn't interfered in the first place, I wouldn't be in this position now."

"So what?" Lupu asked heatedly. "Do you expect people to just stand by and let others die? You deserved every chance at life, even if the results aren't what you might have wanted. Then there's your family. It's bad enough that they will have to cope with your change almost as much as you do. How much worse would it be for them to have lost you entirely? How could you be so selfish as to not consider *their* feelings?"

"Don't bring my family into this, Lupu. I've been a grown boy for years now, and I sure don't need my parents leading me around by the hand anymore."

"You could have fooled me. I've offered you the best solution available and you refuse to even try. And don't give me that crap about it being hard to accept. I *know* it's hard, but nothing major is ever achieved without some sacrifice." Lupu's demeanour softened for a moment. "Heaven knows that I made my own mistakes there. I should have stood up for myself back when I was accused of murdering my sister. Instead I took the easy way out and left the pack. At least I'm trying to correct that now, but it's a long and difficult process. That won't stop me from working at it though. I could use some help, however, and I'm no longer too proud to ask for it. What about you? Are you going to let your fears and pride overcome common sense?"

Dale's ire abated. It was true. Only his fears about being penetrated were holding him back. It was the pleading look in Lupu's eyes that settled it for him though. He found himself wanting to please her and any excuse to be with her was good. He mustered up some confidence and gave her a slight smile. "Okay, let's give it a try."

Lupu gave him a huge hug. "Thank you, Dale! You won't regret this, I promise!"

"Umm, what do I do?" he asked uncertainly.

"Leave the rest to me, lover. Just make yourself comfortable on the mattress… yes, that'll do. Move your tail over a little if you can. Perfect!" She laid down next to him, turning to face him, put her arms around his back to pull him closer and gave him a kiss.

Dale responded eagerly, delighted to finally fulfil a need that he hadn't even realised that he had, one that had preceded his current dilemma. He had been so in need of a true companion ever since he was forced to part with his vixen former lover, but had covered it up and buried himself in his career and bachelor activities. Now he had a beautiful female in his arms again, one who wanted him for what he really was and not what he had become. He felt a surge of desire and a release of his pent-up frustrations. His eyes filled with tears from the intensity of the emotions and he nearly crushed the slender wolftaur bitch against his breasts.

Lupu didn't struggle against it. Instead she revelled in it. Once again, Dale was broadcasting all his feelings empathically, still not able to control this new talent. However, this time Lupu knew what was happening, understood his feelings and reciprocated with her own which he in turn picked up. They remained locked together for a couple of minutes, immersing themselves in the pleasure of the shared feelings. Eventually though they had to break and they panted hard for a while, smiling knowingly at each other.

Dale was the first to speak. "I thought that you intended to use that thing and mount me straight away?"

"I told you that I wanted you to make love to me, not just screw me. I think you preferred it this way, no?"

"Yes!" Dale replied emphatically. "I never thought that I'd find someone to replace my Mary-Anne. I hope that maybe you can be that one."

"Gladly, Dale!" Lupu said, hugging him again.

Dale laughed, the first honest and joyful laugh since this whole episode had begun. Experimentally, he lick-kissed Lupu, finding it both strange and wonderful. She responded immediately and soon they were trading licks at a furious rate, interspersed with delighted giggles. Then their hands started roaming over each other's body, seeking out the pleasure spots. Lupu drew in a sharp breath as his hands stroked hir sensitive nipples and Dale grinned knowingly. He lowered his muzzle to one breast and licked the nipple into rigidity before sucking on it. Lupu whined in pleasure. With one hand, she pulled his head harder to her breast while the other hand sifted the fur at the junction of Dale's upper and lower torsos. Dale revelled in the feelings her attentions elicited and was startled to find himself purring. The two continued this for several minutes, unwilling to wind up this moment of mutual pleasure. Lupu reluctantly brought it to a halt though, feeling that the most propitious moment had arrived.

"Do you think you're ready now, Dale?" she asked.

He paused for a few moments to compose his thoughts, then replied, "No, not really, but I doubt that I could ever be truly ready. Let's give it a try. What do we do next?"

Lupu gave him a mischievous grin. "Why, the fun starts right away, of course. I want you to put the harness onto me first." She handed him the strap-on and turned so that her hindquarters were facing him. She lifted her tail invitingly. Dale grinned back, his mind finally taken off his own body and firmly onto hers. Lupu lifted one foot. "Slip one loop over my leg... yes, that's the way. Now the other. Can you guess what's next?"

Dale realised that the final securing strap could not be tightened into place until one end of the dildo was out of the way. His eyes widened. "You mean...?" Lupu nodded eagerly, knowing what he was going to ask. He went on, "Are you quite, well, *wet* enough?"

"Hell! I've been wet enough since that big kiss! Now do it! Please!!"

She almost pleaded with him, and he complied delightedly. He carefully put the tip of the dildo between her labia, then gave it a push. It slipped in with only modest resistance, accompanied by a slight gasp of pleasure from the wolftaur. Dale grinned as Lupu looked back and gave him a wink. He then tightened the final strap. "What now?"

"The hardest part, for you. Make yourself comfortable on the mattress and lift your tail out of the way. I'm sure you can imagine what I mean."

Dale all too clearly did know but he nevertheless did so. However, another attack of nerves hit him when he looked back to see Lupu getting into position behind him, the artificial erection of the dildo clearly visible between her hind legs. "Lupu, I'm not sure about this."

Instead of proceeding with the mounting, Lupu came beside him and gave him a cuddle. "I know, love. Remember, think of it as making male love to me in an imaginative way. I want this first experience to be a good one so that you won't have the same problems the next time. I'll try to be as careful as I can though. Shall we give it a try? You *must* be willing to accept me. Chakats cannot be penetrated sexually unless they make a conscious decision to allow it, even when they're on heat."

Dale nodded wordlessly, then braced himself. Lupu grabbed his tail, lifting it out of the way, and straddled his prone lower torso. It wasn't easy to do it by herself, but she managed to put the tip of the dildo against Dale's slightly swollen femsex, eliciting a small gasp from him as a thrill raced through his body.

"Relax, Dale. You're too tense." Lupu waited until she could sense him relax enough to allow her inside, then she thrust the dildo firmly and buried its shaft halfway into his vagina. Dale yelped loudly, startled by the feeling of something intruding within his body. His repressed fears exploded upon him and he started shaking violently. Lupu settled down on his lower torso and reached around his upper torso to hug him. She murmured soothingly, not doing anything more about the dildo until he calmed down. Finally, the attack abated and Dale looked over his shoulder, tears streaming from his eyes.

"I'm okay now," he said shakily.

"Are you sure, dear? We can take this as slowly as you want."

"I'm sure. Let's do it!"

"Okay." Lupu drew back slightly, then pushed the dildo the rest of the way into Dale's vagina.

He had tensed, but a moment later realised that pleasure signals from that area were overcoming the feeling of violation. Lupu's efforts to prepare him for the event had not been in vain and he began to relax completely. Lupu looked at him with concern but was reassured by a wink and a small smile from Dale. She decided to go ahead with her efforts. Drawing back again, she gave him a few experimental thrusts, the resistance it encountered serving to pivot the other end deeply into her own vagina. The two shared a groan of pleasure.

"Ooh! I can feel your presence in me, Dale. Push back against my thrusts and pleasure me more!"

Dale gladly complied and for a few minutes they thrusted and moaned in mutual rapture. Having finally accepted the pleasure that being mounted could give him, Dale would have gladly continued doing just that for a lot longer, but his newly acquired body had other ideas. With a speed that caught him unawares, orgasm descended upon him with a vengeance. A long yowl burst from his throat as his limbs stiffened in response to the enormous wave of ecstasy that burst from the area of his vagina and spread through his body. For seconds that seemed like ages, he was in the grip of the most incredible physical pleasure that he had ever known. Finally the wave broke and he was left gasping. Panting hard, he could only stare at Lupu in incredulous wonder as she grinned back at him.

"Felt good, didn't it?" she said. You were broadcasting your orgasm so strongly that I could feel it too. You made me come at the same time, lover, although I don't know whether you could have noticed it in your condition."

At last Dale had enough breath back to say, "That was... *incredible*! Is sex always like that for females?"

"Hmmm, a bit hard to say, but I reckon it was that strong for you because you're in heat and it was your very first experience. However, I can say that I always get a real blast out of it. You outdid me *this* time, but I intend that there be many more opportunities to try my luck."

"I'll gladly give you those opportunities!" Dale said fervently, his fears having been completely wiped out by the intensity of the experience.

"Then I want one right now!" Lupu demanded.

Dale laughed and complied with delight. The next twenty minutes or so was spent in mutual gratification of their desires. Eventually, after several slightly lesser orgasms, Dale declared that he had had enough. Lupu crawled into his arms and the two lovers spent several more minutes just enjoying the afterglow of their efforts. Finally Lupu asked, "How do you feel now? Is being in heat still a problem?"

Dale laughed. "Nope. You took care of that nicely. I suppose the desire will come back, but for now I'm a contented kitty." He paused a moment, then continued, "Thank you, Lupu. Thanks for not letting me give in to my fears. Thanks for tending to my needs when I most needed it."

"You're truly welcome, Dale. Chakat heat lasts for most of two days. I know that it will come back at least once, probably twice before it's over. If you need me again, don't hesitate to ask."

"Oh, I won't, believe me! In fact, I think I need you right now!"

Lupu was a little puzzled. "I thought you said that you were satisfied?"

"What I meant was that my female cravings have been taken care of. Now that my mind is reasonably back to normal, my original libido is reasserting itself. My gorgeous wolftaur lover, how would you like be *really* mounted?"

Lupu's face split in a huge smile. "Oh, yes! If you're up to it, so am I!"

"Oh, I'm *up* to it alright!" Dale replied.

Lupu didn't need further explanation to know exactly *what* was up. She turned around to let Dale get at the harness that she still was wearing. It took only moments to get it off and she eagerly waved hir backside at Dale. He wasted little time in taking up her offer. Only his unfamiliarity with the way his new form handled slowed their coupling, but soon they were one and Dale put his new male equipment to the test. Suffice to say that the results satisfied them both!

* * *

"How are things going in there?" Goldfur asked Forestwalker. The two had been concerned about how Dale was taking Lupu's ministrations and Forest had settled down in the room next door. Shi had a higher empathic Talent level than Goldfur and was easily able to monitor their guest's emotional state from there.

Forest gave hir sister a lascivious grin. "He's doing more than fine. Hell! Between them, those two have given me a case of raging horniness! Whatever exactly Lupu did, it was just the right thing. He's no longer bothered by being in heat, and both are very happy right now."

Goldfur nodded and smiled. "In that case, I think that you can stop checking on them now. As for being horny, I think I can help you out there. Don't forget that *I'm* on heat too!"

Forestwalker got up and gave hir soulmate sister a cuddle. "Thanks, Goldie. What'll we do about Dale later though? Should we tell Dr Gladstone about this?"

"I think that Lupu is doing a better job of helping Dale than we are right now. I propose that we leave it that way for the moment. As for Gladstone, I think that's purely up to Dale to decide. In fact, I think we've intruded enough on his and Lupu's privacy as it is. Let's go to my den and have some personal time of our own. I think I may have lost a denmate today and I need a little cheering up too."

Arm in arm, the two walked down the hall to Goldfur's room. Goldfur may have indeed lost Lupu to Dale this day, but both knew that neither would ever lack for love and caring while the other lived.

As for Dale, another hurdle had been overcome and he now saw that new possibilities were opening up. Perhaps they weren't ones that he had ever considered or liked, but the future no longer looked so bleak to him, not with the possibility of having Lupu by his side to help him through. As he laid next to the wolftaur, cuddling up to her after their lovemaking, he couldn't help wondering though how she'd feel about having a human mate if events in the future brought that to pass. By her cleverness and her genuine affection, she had finally managed to get him to accept this chakat form for now, with all the physical differences that implied, but he had not completely buried his hopes that he would one day walk on two legs again instead of four.

PART THREE
P.O.V. : Dale

I put the flimsy top on, clipping the near-invisible fastener together up front, then adjusting it slightly so my breasts felt comfortable. It was so low-cut that it barely covered my nipples, and it showed *all* my cleavage. Checking it out in the mirror, it looked as if it would fall off at any moment, something that it was undoubtedly meant to do, but it was actually very well designed and hugged my ample bosom firmly and securely.

"Darlin', you do that top justice like few others could."

I turned towards the voice. Lupu regarded me appreciatively. She was a wolftaur bitch with a wild beauty that my more civilised nature found appealing, and she was wearing a blouse that didn't leave much to the imagination either. She came over and gave me a hug.

I kissed her. "Thanks, dear, although I think most chakats would look good in this."

"Perhaps, but *you're* the one wearing it. Besides, it always reminds me of the day we found it."

I nodded as I cast my mind back to that day, not too long after the change.

*   *   *

"Are you going to keep wearing that one top until it falls apart?" Lupu asked me.

I shrugged. "What else do you suggest? I don't have any clothes that weren't given to me by one of the chakats, and I don't have money to go buy my own. My wallet was lost in the transformation also, along with all my teller cards. I can't afford to buy anything yet."

"Not any more!" She held up a package. "This just arrived for you. The courier told me that it was important that you get these as it contains all your documentation, replacement credit and debit cards…"

She stopped talking as I nearly snatched the package from her hands and started opening it. Her grin told me that she had anticipated that response and probably had something else in mind when I was done. I ignored her for the moment. Until now, there had been nothing to prove to the various bureaucracies that I was who I claimed to be, and I couldn't even access the money that I had in my savings accounts. Suddenly, I was no longer a nobody any more and with these I could now stop living on the charity of my benefactors.

Lupu touched my arm to get my attention. "Now, about that top; don't you think we should do something about getting you something to add to your wardrobe?"

I grinned, knowing that I had walked right into her trap. I could see a shopping expedition in mind. For a few days, she and the chakats had been encouraging me to get out of the house and get back into society. I had been resisting the idea, not yet comfortable to confront the world in my new form. However, now I had a reason for going out and I knew that I'd be at the mercy of my wolftaur companion. She wasted no time.

"Borrow a waist pouch and put what you need in it and let's go!" she said, not giving me a choice.

I didn't have a problem getting a pouch from Goldfur, and I put in just about everything. I noted with bemusement that the cards with a photo I.D. had had my human face replaced with that of Goldfur's. I realised that I would have had a bloody hard time convincing someone that that human was really me. One of the cards was my ground vehicle driver's licence. I snorted in contempt. I couldn't drive a normal vehicle with my current body, and I would have to re-learn how to drive in the taur-modified versions if I remained stuck in this body. Needless to say, that card was left on my bedside drawers.

I met Lupu at the front door. She had put on one of her *going-out-to-the-mall* tops. When she visited places like that, she tended to like wearing eye-catching outfits, and this red jacket was no different. It was rather short and only two buttons kept it closed. This resulted in her breasts being firmly pushed together to give people a nice view of cleavage. She wanted people to look, and I was happy to oblige. I still only had one of the plain T-shirts that I wore to preserve my modesty. A rather purposeless thing in this household, I knew, but I still wasn't ready to walk around bare-breasted, especially with *this* rack!

When we got to the local shopping complex, we visited the automatic teller machine first. I got a surprise when I checked my balance. It was substantially higher than I thought it could be. I wasn't exactly a great saver, yet here was a rather large source of funds to draw upon. Later I learned that this was because the Star Corps had deposited some accident compensation benefits into the account, and this was only the *interim* pay-out. I was now fairly well-off! This didn't escape Lupu, of course, and it wasn't long before we were headed to the clothes shops. She took me to her favourite stores and made me try on several items. Despite my fears, she had a practical mind, and she chose some very suitable tops to suit my tastes. After choosing a couple of simple halters, a prettily patterned T-shirt and a nice blouse, a smart jacket caught my eye. Although it was cut for a female, it appealed more to my masculine personality. It was a light brown that went well with the golden-brown of my fur. Looking at the result in the mirror, I was very pleased with it. Then Lupu held out one more item for me. I hesitated before taking it from her. It was small. Very small. It was the colour of a blue cloudless sky, and weighed about as much. I arched an eyebrow at Lupu questioningly.

Lupu shrugged and gave me a coy smile. "Please?" was all she said.

I considered it, then thought '*What have I gotten myself into? Oh, what the hell!*' and put it on. The narrow straps disappeared into my fur and made it look totally self-supporting. Judicious small amounts of darker blue lace adorned it, but otherwise it was beautiful in its simplicity. It barely came up over my milk-swollen nipples, and the figure-hugging material hid them not in the slightest. In fact, the material barely covered a third of my generously sized breasts, and revealed my cleavage totally. Looking in the mirror, I knew that this item had one purpose only, and by the reaction I was having to it, it was fulfilling that purpose admirably. I tore my eyes away from the sight before something unwanted happened right there in public. The shop owner was there, helping Lupu pick out garments for me. When I turned to face the female snow leopard morph, she exclaimed in delight.

"That colour suits you perfectly! Your mate is going to be very pleased!" she remarked.

I didn't bother disabusing her of the notion that Lupu and I were mated. It was hardly surprising that she'd think so, especially considering what we were doing. Then I presented myself to Lupu whose jaw dropped a little in surprised delight. She took a really good look at me, and I let her appraise the effect until she was content. Then she sighed.

"Thank you, Dale. I know that this wasn't what you came in for, and I know that the male part of you is probably uncomfortable about this. However, I was dying to see what you'd look like in that. Thanks for indulging me, hon."

I smiled back at her. "True, I wouldn't ever choose this for myself, but I have to admit that it suits me well. So, you like it?" Lupu nodded eagerly. "Good! I wouldn't want to think that I had wasted my money."

Lupu's jaw dropped in surprise. "You're buying it?" she asked incredulously.

"Yep." I answered simply.

"Not that I object, but why?"

"Just because you like it and it pleases me to indulge you. I'm very grateful for all you've done for me so far. Consider it a way of paying you back a little."

Lupu threw her arms around me, hugging and lick-kissing me thoroughly. I laughed and gave her a few licks back. I took great delight in pleasing her. The shop owner was so happy with all the garments that I'd bought there that she threw in a pretty tail ribbon as a bonus. Lupu would have to show me how to use that!

We walked out of that shop with quite a haul. Somehow I wouldn't be surprised if I ended up back there again in the near future. Lupu had bought a new halter too. Not that she needed another as she had quite a collection. However, I knew that being female, that fact wouldn't stop her! She was a little surprised at how much that I had bought though.

"I thought that you didn't like shopping?" she queried.

"I don't," I replied. "However, I always liked to dress smartly as a human, and I still do as a chakat. The actual process of going out and trying on all those items of apparel is tedious to me, but I like the results." I paused to push my long tresses out of my eyes for the millionth time. "Now if only I could do something about this annoying hair!" I said with a touch of irritation.

"Easily fixed!" exclaimed Lupu, grabbing my arm and steering me down one of the side aisles.

'*Chez Fur*' proclaimed the sign on the shop window. '*Hair and fur styling*' it said underneath.

"This is my favourite hairdresser," Lupu said. "If Mademoiselle Hephzibah can't help you find something to your taste, no one can!

Hephzibah proved to be a Persian Cat morph. Her luxuriously long fur was meticulously styled and adorned with various ribbons and such. She took one look at my waist-long hair and exclaimed, "Ooooh! Vhat *marvellous* hair you have, ma Cherie! What is ze magic zat you wish me to work upon eet?"

Lupu didn't give me a chance to answer. "Dale would love to have something elegantly simple, Hephzibah dear. Cut it to just below the shoulders and dye it. Auburn, I think."

Hephzibah looked slightly disappointed. "But such theengs I could do with zis. Eet would be a shame not to make it a work of art."

I began to feel a little panicky. There was no way that I wanted to spend hours in this place and walk out with some ghastly hair-do. I worried too much though. Lupu had her firmly under control though and wouldn't let her get carried away.

"No, love. Dale doesn't go in for that kind of thing. I have confidence in your ability to make hir wonderful with the simplest of styles." I noticed Lupu's use of the herm pronoun then. She'd been using the male ones for me, but I realised that it was much easier to simply let Hephzibah think that I was a regular chakat rather than trying to explain my peculiar circumstances.

Hephzibah was mollified by the praise of her abilities and led me off to one of the work areas. She personally cut my hair and I was amazed at how much lighter my head felt as hank after hank of golden hair fell to the floor. Then swiftly and skilfully, she began to shape it, all the while chattering at me in that outrageous French accent. I had no idea how much of it was real and how much was an affectation, but at least it seemed that she was quite prepared to make it a one-sided conversation, which spared me from having to comment on any of the stuff that she talked about, most of which went straight in one ear and out the other. Then she had me lean over a basin and gave me a thorough shampoo. Next she carefully but firmly put a waterproof band around my hairline and then chose a hair dye colour.

"A lighter shade of brown would suit you best, with just ze hint of red to match your fur, I think!

With a flourish, she presented the bottle to me with the sample on front. I shrugged, not really knowing any better. Some time later, the dye job complete and my hair brushed, shaped and dried, I was shown the result in the mirror. My jaw dropped. I was stunned by the result. At last, something other than Goldfur's visage gazed back at me. The result was good... bloody good! I realised then that Lupu had been right to choose this place. Even someone like me could see that for all her flamboyancy, Hephzibah sure knew what she was doing. I thanked the Mademoiselle profusely, her smile telling me that this was exactly what she craved. Of course, a fairly hefty fee was needed too, but I found that I didn't mind a bit. My head felt freer, the hair no longer got in my way at all, and I no longer could be mistaken for Goldfur. I walked back to the PTV feeling rather good about myself.

Lupu said, "You look scrumptious, love. Aren't you glad that I brought you here now?"

"Of course I am. I'd be an idiot if I said otherwise. What now though?"

"How about lunch first?"

I suddenly realised that I was ravenous and nodded eagerly. After dropping off our purchases, I treated Lupu to a meal at the nearby Garden Café. As usual, I was impressed with the sheer amount of food that the chakat form could put away. One advantage of that though was that I could get to try out several different dishes. Something that I had noticed from the first day of my change was the subtle difference in how everything tasted to me now. Every dish therefore was a totally new experience to me and I thoroughly enjoyed it.

When we were finally replete, Lupu asked me, "What would you like to do next?"

I thought for a moment, but it wasn't hard to decide. "Take me to my apartment."

Lupu was startled, and I realised that the thought that I actually had a residence somewhere else than at Goldfur's place had never crossed her mind. She nodded. "Okay. I'm curious to see what you call home."

"You'll be disappointed. It's nothing special."

"Let me be the judge of that," she replied.

I shrugged. *Let her form her own opinions.* Driving to my apartment took about half an hour; going to the shopping complex had already taken us in roughly the right direction. The building occupied a small but neatly landscaped lot planted with shrubs and small trees. On the way up the stairs I stumbled. It gave me pause; as a human I'd gone up a thousand times without a thought. I opened the door for Lupu and stepped in behind her. Even with only two chairs and the entertainment console in it, the lounge room felt cramped. I found myself stepping carefully to avoid bumping into things.

Suddenly a vase toppled over with a crash, dislodged by my tail. "Crap!" I snarled, turning about not *quite* quickly enough to prevent the vase from rolling off onto the floor.

"What's that?" Lupu inquired.

"Oh, just something I picked up during a tour," I replied. Shelves loaded with knick-knacks I'd picked up while on various duty assignments lined three walls. "Um," I mumbled, feeling momentarily faint as a thought crossed my mind. The latest batch

of souvenirs, originally destined to join the collection, had instead become a part of my new body.

After waiting a moment for Lupu to examine the shelves I showed her the rest of the place. A kitchen-dinette, a single bedroom, and a bathroom (with a toilet that I could barely use now) completed the layout. Stairs lead down to a laundry next to the storeroom and garage. I noticed that in addition to looking at things, she also sniffed them. I tried it myself and became aware of a wealth of scents I could detect, if not identify. One particular odour jumped out at me. With a shock I realised that it was the scent of my own former body!

"Small, but nice," Lupu commented. "Anything you want to take back?"

I nodded, then I grabbed some documents, filled a bag with most of my favourite music disks, took my personal PADD and a few other knick-knacks that I felt like having. For a moment I stared at the clothes and shoes in my wardrobe, tempted to fling the footwear out the window. I restrained myself and grabbed a jacket only. Trying it on, I found that the formerly large and roomy garment was now barely big enough to fit my powerful new form. I thought that I would feel at home here, but instead I felt awkward and out of place. My body didn't fit and I kept bumping into furniture and corners. The heights of the benches seemed wrong, and I almost laughed out loud at the thought of squeezing this body onto my single bed. Sadly, what had been my home was now merely a place that stored my possessions.

"Let's get out of here," I told Lupu.

"It's no longer home, is it?" she deduced shrewdly.

"You're right. This is a human's home, and no place for people like us."

I saw her lift an eyebrow as she noted my choice of words, but she didn't say any more. She helped me carry out the bags I'd filled, then I closed and locked the door. I didn't really know when I'd bother coming back. If the scientists managed to do the impossible, then I could come back here again, but not now. It hurt too much.

* * *

It was amazing the difference that day's activities made. Everyone at the den could now see me as an individual instead of Goldfur's clone. I suddenly felt like a new person, rather than a human masquerading as someone else. It's staggering how much of ourselves we store in such slight things. I took pride in maintaining my new looks, and now that I had many of my important personal items with me, I could indulge in a few things I hadn't been able to up until then. I was an individual person again, both in the eyes of my hosts and in that of the public. Life still had a lot of uncertainties in store for me, but I felt better equipped to handle them now.

The following days consisted of more practice with my body's capabilities, talking to the various big brains from Star Corps, and getting more seemingly pointless tests done. Also, I began to swing my weight in the household. Rather than be a constant burden on them, I volunteered to do various chores. Cub-minding was one that I was least adept at, but was most appreciated, freeing up their parents to do other more pressing tasks. This activity brought about one of the next significant changes in my attitudes. For once, I was almost alone in the house. Only Trina remained, working in her office. I'd been left in charge of the youngest cub and I felt quite honoured by the trust that they had in me. However, when Tailstalker started mewling constantly, I was at a bit of a loss at how to placate hir. It slowly got through my thick head that the empathic abilities of my new body were telling me exactly what was wrong. Shi was hungry! I got completely flustered. Shi wanted to be fed much sooner than normal, but the chakats didn't have anything like a baby's bottle in the place! I was about to seek out Trina's help when a thought occurred to me. There was one other source of milk! I was stunned that I even considered it, but I knew that the milk in my own breasts would be perfect. I dithered for way too long, but Tailstalker's ever-increasingly loud mewling finally pushed me over the edge. I thanked God that I was alone because I was sure that I couldn't do what I was about to do with an audience. I unfastened the halter I was wearing, picked up Tailstalker, then placed her muzzle near one breast. Hir tiny little hands reached out to grasp the fur on my left breast as shi pulled hir muzzle straight to the nipple. Without any hesitation, she started suckling upon the teat, and I gasped at the sensation. It felt *good*! *Really* good! I knew what it felt like to have the milk flow due to Lupu's marvellous ministrations, but this was different. There was something extra this time. Then I realised what it was. I could feel the cub's pleasure at being fed, and my empathic senses were passing that on to me. I closed my eyes and just soaked it up. No wonder chakats loved breastfeeding their children so much. I purred and purred.

"I think shi's done," said a familiar voice after a long time. I opened my eyes and saw Trina's gently smiling face in front of me. I was not in the slightest bit bothered by being discovered. I finally understood the reasons behind the attitudes of the various residents of this den, and I suddenly realised that I now shared them. I held Tailstalker up to Trina who carefully took the sleeping cub from me and placed hir in the crib. She bent over the child and kissed hir on the forehead. I took a moment to watch her do so. As always, she wore nothing about the den, and the beautiful white-furred femme looked exceptionally nice. For the first time, I did not avert my eyes in embarrassment. I took the time to look her over carefully. I was still looking when she straightened up and turned around. She realised what I was doing and grinned, pulling a few poses for me. Instead of being hopelessly embarrassed, I took what she offered and enjoyed the view before we both broke into quiet laughter as her antics got more and more silly. She held out a hand to me and I got up and left the room with her.

"You did that well," Trina said when we reached the living area.

"Thanks," I replied. "That was quite an experience."

"We'll make a real chakat out of you yet!" she added. Startled, I realised that she might be right. She added, "However, won't that upset your plans to wean yourself?"

I shrugged helplessly. "It had to be done. Besides, now that I know fully what it's like, I'm not so sure any more that I want to wean myself."

Trina laughed loudly at that. "Yes, I can certainly understand that. Welcome to the mothers' club."

I wasn't quite sure how to respond to that, so I simply smiled in agreement. Then Trina startled me by kissing me.

"That's for a job well done, Dale. Feel free to explore more of your new nature with me sometime." With that, she turned away and strolled off to her office, hips swaying, tail swishing. I knew damn well that it was done for my benefit, and I wondered if I was ready for that aspect of this extended family yet.

*   *   *

Goldfur disappeared along with hir cubs the next day. Apparently shi had left to rejoin hir mate, Garrek, who had been spending time in his home village attending to clan business. That left fewer cubs to look after, and more time on my hands, and I used it to help Trina in the office whenever I wasn't busy practising new techniques with my body or talking to Dr Gladstone. I must admit to being sceptical about the psych services until this incident, but he managed to help me with such competent ease that I would be forever in his debt. I forgot to ask him though about how I should feel when Garrek returned to his home here until the moment he walked in. He was such a striking sight. I had never seen such a big foxtaur before, nor one so boldly coloured. However, those weren't the things that were bothering me. As soon as I laid eyes on him, I felt like an intruder in his territory. I knew it was because my male psyche saw him as a rival male, but that didn't make it any easier to deal with. It didn't help to realise that he'd probably been informed about me and wouldn't be too surprised to finally meet me; I still felt as if I was a usurper in his home. I was very nervous when he stepped up to greet me.

"Hello there! You must be Dale. I'm pleased to meet you."

Although they were standard lines, he said them with a genuineness that wasn't a mere affectation. I knew immediately that here was a person as honest and straightforward as any other member of this family, which shouldn't have come as a surprise to me. Still, I just stood there dumbly, not knowing what to do until Lupu gave me a nudge in the ribs with her elbow. That jolted me out of stasis and I held out my hand to shake his.

"Same here, Garrek. I hope that I'm not in the way or anything."

"Don't worry about it. You're hardly the first unusual addition to this madhouse, and I strongly suspect that you won't be the last. At least the haircut and dye job will stop me from doing anything mutually embarrassing."

I nodded in fervent agreement. "So, what have you been up to? The others have been remarkably tight-lipped about that."

Garrek took my arm and guided me to a corner of the living room. I noticed that he seemed a little embarrassed and wondered why my question should elicit that response. He took a bottle of soft drink from the small bar fridge and asked me if I wanted one. I accepted, mostly out of sociability rather than thirst and he then sat down on a lounging cushion. I took one nearby and we both took swigs out of the bottles. I realised that he was getting himself in the mood to talk. Finally he spoke.

"I've been fulfilling a clan obligation, one that has opened my eyes a little better to my own culture, but still involves a certain degree of uncomfortableness for me." He then gave me a synopsis of the past several days events. I learned for the first time that foxtaur vixens outnumbered the males three to one, thus making males very valuable for breeding purposes. He had been required to provide such services for a week, and he was usually a rather quiet and reserved person outside of his own family, so he found the task rather daunting. (*NOTE: See the story – Tales of the Foxtaur Clans #5: Obligation – for the full details.*)

I wondered why he was telling me all this at first, then I realised what the reason probably was. He'd been briefed on my circumstances and he was doing his bit to get my mind off my plight, or to show that others had problems too. On top of this, I sensed a certain amount of male camaraderie. He was treating me as the man I had been, rather then the chakat that I presently was. I knew that *I* couldn't have made that distinction so quickly. I decided that Garrek was a very perceptive person and warmed up to him a lot, and soon we were chatting like old friends.

* * *

For a few days, I felt almost at home. It felt like I was more like a visiting relative rather than a charity case. I kept myself busy and helped where I could. Then one morning, Forestwalker came up to me and let me know what was going to be happening soon. Shi drew me aside and then carefully made hirself comfortable. I realised with a start that shi was extremely gravid. I mean, I had always known that shi was pregnant and the cub wasn't going to be long in coming, but until that moment I hadn't really realised just how close.

"Dale, tomorrow I'm due to give birth to this cub," shi started, patting hir swollen belly. "As is our custom, we're having a birthing party, and many of my relatives will be attending. I need to know if you're going to have a problem with this."

"You can pinpoint the birth that accurately?" I asked curiously.

"To the day, yes. It's rare that we miss."

I thought about the situation a bit, then asked, "Will you be letting them know about my circumstances?"

"Only if you let us. We'll respect your privacy, but if you choose to stick around, we can make things easier for you if you let us tell them about you. Otherwise we can arrange for you to stay elsewhere until this is all over if you can't cope."

"If your relatives promise not to blab, I reckon that I can deal with it for a while. I might have to retreat to the bedroom if it gets too much for me, but I doubt it. I've always enjoyed parties."

Forestwalker grinned at that. "I don't think you fully understand what our birthing parties are like. You could soon find out though. I'd be honoured if you joined us at the event."

"The honour's mine," I replied. "I'd be pleased to attend."

Forestwalker held up a hand to stop me talking. "Not so fast! I think you'd better know what you'd be letting yourself in for first. This is an invitation to actually be present at the birth, as well as celebrating afterwards."

My jaw dropped. Now *that* I hadn't counted on. Forestwalker grinned. "I thought that might give you a surprise. It's much nicer than you think though. It's nothing like the sterile atmosphere of a delivery room that humans seem to prefer for some reason. You don't have to give me your decision now, but I think you'll find it interesting."

"No, I don't think I need more time to consider my answer. I've prided myself on my ability to deal with new situations, although my transformation rather strained that. As I said, I'd be honoured to be present at the birth of your cub. Got any more surprises for me though?"

Shi smiled hugely at that. "Probably, but nothing that you won't be able to handle, I think. Thank you for accepting. Now there are other matters to deal with. Some of the family will be staying overnight, and rooms are at a premium already. We won't kick you out of your room though, but if you volunteer to spend at least one night sharing it with another, we'd be very grateful. If you're inclined, I think Lupu would be happy to move in for a night or two."

I looked at hir sharply, but the smile never dimmed. I sighed and asked, "Is there any time when you aren't scheming something to throw us together?"

"Why, Dale, I don't know what you mean!" shi exclaimed with a great show of fake sincerity. I growled and shi giggled. "Okay. Honestly, it's the best arrangement anyway, but I can't help thinking that you should take advantage of the situation."

I gave up on saying anything else. I had already learned one thing about chakats: they totally lacked a sense of jealousy. None. Zilch. They barely even understood the concept. They had nothing against the concept of monogamy, but they couldn't understand why their ability to love should be restricted to only one if they met someone else deserving of it. They saw that Lupu liked me, and despite the fact that she was already Goldfur's mate, they felt that we made a good pairing and I'd been feeling their subtle (and now their not-so-subtle) manipulations to bring us together more. "Okay, if she says she wants to, I'll go along with that."

"Thanks, Dale. She already said yes. The first of the guests will be arriving today, including my parents and the Admiral. We'll have to warn my mother and sire about you because your scent's the same as Goldfur's. It could be very disconcerting otherwise."

"Naturally," I agreed, "But who's this Admiral?"

Forestwalker got up. "Why, the cub's sire, of course. Can't have a birthing without the sire to share the moment, can I?" Shi smiled and started to walk off.

"Wait! You've only ever referred to the cub's sire as 'Boyce' before. I didn't know that he, or shi was an admiral." With a name like that, I had been completely in the dark as to the nature of the sire's parentage. It didn't sound like a chakat name, but neither did it sound like that of any other taur species' style of naming that I knew about, and I knew enough about chakats to know that they could only interbreed with other taur species. It had me puzzled.

"Oh yes, he's an admiral in Star Fleet. Boyce Garald Kline Jr. And he's human."

Okay, just as I thought I'd gotten over being shocked, shi did it to me again. My jaw dropped and I was dumbfounded. "But..." I began.

Forestwalker interrupted me. "But humans can't interbreed with taurs, not even lusty chakats. Well, this one can due to a gift from an elder race, and as soon as we realised that fact, we conceived a cub as soon as possible. It's not even his first chakat hybrid. Midnight bore the first. Ember is his daughter."

Shi left me thinking about that one. I'd been occasionally breastfeeding the daughter of an admiral? The cub was being slowly weaned, but the chakats let their cubs suckle at the breast for up to two years, and feeding them that way provided comfort and security that was irreplaceable. I wondered what an admiral would think of a lowly ensign feeding his precious child. I soon found out. About two hours later, the comm rang and Forestwalker answered it. I heard hir excited voice call out, "He's here!" before shi made a beeline for the backyard. I wondered about that and curiously followed hir. I quickly became aware of a humming sound growing, one that was familiar to me. I soon spotted the shuttle that was headed in our direction. That *had* to be the Admiral's. Not too many people could get permission to land a shuttle in a suburban backyard; not even one as big as this yard. By the time he brought the small vessel in to a textbook landing, a small crowd had gathered to welcome him. The door had barely a chance to open before Ember streaked into the gap. A moment later, a tall and handsome male human dressed in a Star Fleet uniform stepped out with the cub in his arms, hir tiny tongue furiously licking him in greeting kisses. There was absolutely no doubt in my mind now that this was Ember's father. The cubs were never fooled. Shi knew hir father without a doubt. Forestwalker threw hir arms about both and lick-kissed his other cheek. Then they kissed human-style, long and lovingly. Midnight was next, then Goldfur. Finally, it was my turn to be introduced. I felt like disappearing into the shadows or something. He might be in Star Fleet and me in the Star Corps, but we were both part of the Space Services, and he was technically my superior officer.

"Judging by your resemblance to Goldfur," he said when we came face-to-face, "You must be Dale."

I threw him my best salute. "Yes, sir! Ensign Dale Perkins, sir."

"At ease, Dale! Neither of us are on duty here, and we're amongst family." He stuck out his hand. "A pleasure to meet you, anyway. I've heard a lot of good things about you."

I shook his hand with great relief. "Thank you, sir… I mean… ummm… What *do* I call you then?!"

"Boyce will do fine here. Now, please excuse me. I have a lot of catching up to with mates."

I nodded and he turned away into the arms of a chakat. I could feel their pleasure and anticipation already. Only then did I notice a Caitian amongst the crowd. She must have been there for a while, but I hadn't noticed her get out of the shuttle. She caught my eye and smiled before turning back to the conversation she was having with Midnight. I noticed the rank pips on her uniform's collar and realised that she must be the Admiral's second in command. I had to wonder what she was doing here, although judging by the familiarity which she and the others seemed to have, she must be a regular visitor. Then a thought occurred to me. Boyce now had children by two chakats so far, which meant that he probably shared the same easy relationships with the entire family, just the way chakats did. After all, he did say *mates*, and I was almost certain he wasn't using the Australian term for friends. Could she be yet another in the family? I soon found out.

The Admiral finished his round of cuddles and greetings and turned back to me. "Dale! I fear I've been a bit remiss in my introductions." He beckoned the Caitian over. "Rosepetal, I'd like to introduce you to Goldfur's doppelganger, Dale Perkins. Dale, this is my First Wife, Commander Rosepetal Silpurr." He reached down and plucked a furball from amongst a wrestling bundle of playful cubs, revealing what appeared to be a young female Caitian child. "And this is our daughter, Kayla."

"D-a-d! Lemme down!" objected Kayla. Boyce did so and she immediately rejoined the scrum.

I was really bemused now. Boyce not only had chakat children, but one from an alien also? He could have meant she was an adopted child, but frankly I didn't consider that possibility for more than a moment. Not after seeing the same hazel eyes as her father, anyway; completely unlike her mother's golden yellow ones. I *had* to learn more about him!

The crowd drifted off in the direction of the house and into the living room. The kids were left to work off the abundant energy that they seemed to have unleashed when their visitor arrived. I parked myself in a corner out of the way and let the conversation roll around me, soaking up some relevant details. Typical of chakats though, they didn't let me get away with being unsociable for long and I soon found myself detailing my recent experiences to the Admiral and his wife. I was beginning to run dry when Lupu interrupted with an announcement of lunch. Now if there's anything that a chakat loves only slightly less than sex, it's a good meal. There was a virtual stampede for the dining table, and I was amused to note that the Admiral definitely was *not* the last to get there. There's nothing like a good feed with good company. That above all else helped me to become comfortable in Boyce's presence.

*   *   *

I suppose that by now I should be used to being wrong. Just as I think that I've got things figured out, or that I won't be surprised again, these people proved otherwise. The birthing party started off much as I expected it to. Various relatives arrived in a steady stream. Forest and Goldfur's parents were amongst the earliest. I was on hand for most of the welcomes because not only did it give me a chance to be introduced to so many people all at once, but it also let my hosts head off any misunderstandings. Some jumped to the conclusion that I was Goldfur with a new hairstyle the moment they scented me. Of course, when Goldfur was also there, it merely meant some amusing confusion.

When the majority had arrived, we settled down in the living room to chat, drink and eat, then chat some more. Having acquiesced to their desire to have me part of the birth, I was now stuck with all the rest too. Not one for so much socialising, I was saved from boredom due to the fact that so many of the chakats had very interesting tales to tell, and because I was fresh meat, they were more than eager to relate them all to me. I barely had time to wonder just exactly when the birth was supposed to take place! That question was eventually answered when a yelp cut through the conversation. With everyone's eyes turned upon hir, Forest's own eyes fairly sparkled as shi announced: "Yes folks, that was the first contraction!" The conversation burst out anew, its volume much increased. I had to wonder, if they always held birthing parties like this, why did they find new births so endlessly fascinating? Perhaps one of these days I'd find out, but not yet.

Eventually the contractions were coming close enough

together for Brightsong, their clan midwife, to declare that it was time for them to move to the nursery. Lupu grabbed my arm and dragged me after Forest. "Come on! We wanna get a good spot to watch!" she said enthusiastically.

I wasn't so sure. I know that I had agreed to attend, but I was now getting a case of cold feet. Then, just to make it worse, I noticed that not one person in that room had any clothing on except me. Some of the chakats in the living room had already been topless, but I knew that their species sometimes didn't bother with such things. "What's going on here?" I whispered to Lupu, my hands on the straps of my halter to indicate what I meant.

"Chakat custom," shi replied. "The cubs come naked into the world, and are innocents. The chakats show that they nurture this innocence and greet their children in a way that shows that they value each new addition to the family and that they will all protect and feed the cub."

"So that means...?" I asked, knowing what the answered would most likely be.

"Get it off!" ordered Lupu with a very big grin on her face.

Trapped, I had little choice but to comply. It felt really weird taking off the halter in front of so many people, but nobody really looked. All their attention was focused on the mother-to-be. I crossed my arms over my breasts, my nerves soothed by that token of modesty. I barely started to calm down when I was well and truly knocked for a loop. Boyce walked into the room, his eyes fixed on his mate. He settled behind Forest and put his arms around hir waist. Shi leant back, turning hir head to give him a big kiss on the cheek, That was hardly surprising. What boggled me though was the fact that he wasn't wearing a stitch of clothing! I felt keenly aware of both our situations, but he seemed oblivious. I just tried to make myself inconspicuous for the rest of the event.

I must admit that it was an interesting experience. I'm

glad that I hadn't known everything beforehand or else I might have chickened out and I would have lost out on some valuable insights into chakat sociology. Watching a cub emerge from hir home of ten and a half months is something that everyone should experience at least once in their lives. After that, the still-damp kitten was presented to the family before Forest took hir to the breast for hir first feed. Only then did the family start leaving the room, the hot topic of debate being prospective names for the child. As it turns out, hir name wasn't formalised for a long time, but in time, shi would come to be known as Windrunner. I had just as much fun discussing names with the other chakats too though while we ate snacks and drinks supplied by Goldfur and Lupu.

It was a couple of hours later before I realised that I hadn't put my top back on!

* * *

The next milestone occurred when my body reached the opposite extreme of its sexual cycle and I went into male rut. It was almost an anti-climax though because at last I was in reasonably familiar territory. Not that I had ever been quite this horny before, but at least I knew what was happening and it didn't conflict with my lifetime experience with sexual desire. I had to be extra careful though not to let it get away from me because if I did, I was stuck with an erection for quite a while, and I had no way to hide it other than lying down until it went away. Needless to say, the first day I spent lying down a lot! I was determined to get some self-control though without help from others, and by the second day, it wasn't so bad. I couldn't give myself all the credit though. Lupu was more than happy to indulge me and take the edge off the cravings. Of course, she often undid the benefits by flirting with me at other times, knowing full well the effect she was having on me. I made a mental note to myself: Lupu might be a kind and helpful person, but she was still a wolftaur bitch with a very independent and forthright demeanour, not to mention a mischievous streak. If she felt interested in me sexually, she didn't bother to hide it.

One thing that didn't change while at the peak of the male cycle was the enjoyment that I felt breastfeeding cubs. Yes, I had soon realised that I was never going to be able to wean myself while living with this family. Everyone now fully trusted me with caring for the cubs in their absence, and I had found out that feeding them was a normal part of that task. Considering the amount of pleasure it gave the carer, I was a bit surprised that they would relinquish that task to me at all, despite the occasional painful nip that such activity sometimes incurred. I wondered if they were deliberately letting me do it to make me feel more useful and get some enjoyment out of my situation. I didn't ask though. I just did the tasks that I was asked to do and thanked them by doing them well.

Another thing that still took me by surprise despite everything that had pointed towards it. Trina had been quite serious in her attitude towards me. While I had assumed that she was only flirting with me as she did with everyone else, I soon found out that she never did anything that she wasn't prepared to follow through with. We had just finished another day's work and Trina had dragged herself away from her office early for a change. Lupu had taken the cubs off my hands and was playing with them out on the grass in the back yard. Trina sat down on the floor next to me and smiled.

"You've been such a great help to me these past few days, Dale. I've managed to get my project done a little earlier than expected. I'd like to show my appreciation."

"You know that there's no need for that, Trina. I'm just glad to be pulling my weight around here."

Trina shook her head. "Nobody expects or demands that you do anything at all, Dale. Goldfur offered hir help unreservedly, and as part of hir extended family, we all honour that commitment. Nevertheless, your willingness to help out is much appreciated, and should be rewarded. Besides, I think what I have in mind will be not only be pleasurable, but beneficial."

Before I could ask what she meant by that, she got up and put her arms around me and lick-kissed my cheek.

"Come join me in my room, dear. I know what your body is going through at the moment, and I'd like to help you there. I promise that you'll enjoy it."

I was a little shocked. Sure, I knew intellectually that Trina was free with her affections, but even so I never expected to be so straight-forwardly propositioned. "But... what about your other mates? What will they think?"

Trina laughed. "So like a human! You keep thinking in such limited terms when it comes to sex. I love my mates dearly, and nothing on Earth will ever change that, but recreational sex has no impact on those relationships anyway. My dear, the most that will happen is that they'll ask me what it was like!" She became semi-serious for a moment. "I enjoy my sex-life, hon, and I intend to do so for a while. However, I never do so with anyone I don't like or trust. I like you a lot, Dale. We all do. Would you give me the pleasure of giving *you* pleasure?"

Not knowing what to say, I just nodded. She smiled and dragged me to my feet, leading me to her room. Now don't think that I hadn't thought about having sex with this gorgeous vixen, because that thought had occurred to me many times over the past several days. My body had changed, but my lusts had not. However, I had never expected to have those fantasies brought to reality. Consequently, I just stood there in her room like an idiot, not really knowing what to do first. She was understanding though and controlled the encounter. She did as promised and gave me a *lot* of pleasure. After bringing me to orgasm though, I was better able to pleasure her in return for the next round. We spent the entire time until Lupu stuck her grinning face in the door to announce that dinner was ready, making love again and again. My hormone charged body was finally sated, but it seemed Trina was as fresh as a daisy. It seemed that descriptions of her legendary endurance weren't exaggerated.

Around the dinner table, conversation went as normal, yet I knew they all knew what had just happened, and they also knew that I knew. I shook my head. Too many 'knews'! The bottom line was that it was totally inconsequential to them. It was the choice of Trina and myself, and none of their business, so they didn't pry. I was grateful for that, not because I was embarrassed about it any more, but because I regarded our encounter as a private special moment just between us. She had more than repaid me for my efforts and I would recall those moments together with pleasure for a long time to come.

*   *   *

It seemed amazing to me then, but I slipped into the routine of the household so smoothly that it was easy to forget about my plight. I had never met such a varied group of people who were just so damn nice! When I wasn't playing cubsitter or something else, I was practising with my new body. I began to wonder why I wasn't feeling more concerned about the length of time without any news concerning my problem. I mean, I still wanted my old body back, but the urgency just wasn't there any more. My mind seemed to be treating this like a vacation away from its normal repose and was quite happy where it was for now. When the heat cycle came back around again, I almost felt eager because it meant spending more intimate time with Lupu. It's funny how you can get used to just about anything if you only give it a chance. I realised that my new body was helping to shape my feelings, but frankly I didn't give a damn any more.

To celebrate my progress, my temporary family decreed that it was time for me to go on a proper outing. Dinner and a movie sounded great to me because I was getting just a little antsy about being confined to the den for most of the time, and I was overcoming my inhibitions about being in public. We decided to go the whole hog and dress formally, thus bringing us to where I began recounting this episode. I must admit that I was feeling quite excited about this evening's outing. A full month had passed since my life had been turned upside down when I was changed into a chakat. I looked at myself in the full length mirror that adorned one side of the walk-in wardrobe. Thirty one days ago, a moderately handsome man had gazed back at me. Now, a golden-furred felitaur filled my view. Also, the light blue of the top went well with my fur, and the figure-hugging fabric showed off my every curve and bump. I grinned. Hell, I was a bloody attractive creature! I may not have ever chosen to be a chakat, but more and more I appreciated this sleek, powerful and beautiful form. In fact, despite having learned some control of this body, I still couldn't look at myself in the mirror for too long without turning myself on.

Lupu gave a howl of appreciation. Okay, it was a small howl, but I liked the sentiment. Satisfied that my top was comfortably in position, I put my jacket on, but left it unbuttoned. No point in having that sexy piece of apparel on if you couldn't see it! I snapped on a belt pouch and I was ready. I offered my arm to Lupu, and then we walked out to join the others.

We all walked into town. The short distance made it a pleasant stroll, and there wasn't any point in taking the PTV. Besides, there were so many of us, we couldn't have all fitted. Goldfur, Garrek, Forestwalker, Midnight, Kris & Trina made up the rest of the party. All the cubs were left in the care of a babysitter. Personally I thought that the babysitter was biting off a lot more than she could chew with all those children, but if the others thought that she could handle it, who was I to disagree?

I admit it. I thoroughly enjoyed the walk. I had expected to feel as if everyone would be staring at me and knowing I was a fraud; a wolf in chakat's clothing so to speak. Of course that was impossible, but I knew I wasn't the most graceful of taurs, and I felt that my clumsiness would stand out like a beacon. It seems that all my practice had paid off though. I had no difficulty at all, and not once did my tail get in the way. Lupu seemed attached to my arm throughout the walk, and she spent most of it pointing out the local sights and helping me to familiarise myself with the neighbourhood. I barely noticed that the various other couples were doing much the same. I suppose that being parents left them little time just to be with each other and they would make the most of occasions like these.

We came to the main street of the quiet township near Goldfur's den. As were many towns built after the Gene Wars, it looked fairly modern and well laid-out. I noted plenty of trees to give shade in the heat of summer and the brightly-themed street-scaping would keep it looking cheery during dull winter days.

Forestwalker said to me, "Most of the restaurants are along this street. Since you're the guest of honour, you get to choose what we eat. Don't worry about our preferences because we've all got pretty broad tastes."

"Okay," I replied. "Let's just stroll down here until something strikes my fancy."

"Fine by us," shi replied.

I passed up a couple of places that looked nice enough because I wanted to see what else this town had to offer. However, when I came to a place named *D.K's Steakhouse*, my appetite suddenly went into overdrive. I had a real hankering for a big sirloin right then. "How about this place?" I asked the others.

Goldfur's expression hardened. Wordlessly shi pointed to an inconspicuous sticker in the bottom left of the window. It was very simple, plain green circle with the letter H and the numeral one in white. I looked at hir in puzzlement.

Goldfur said, "That's the symbol of a *Humans First* sympathiser. People like us... like *you*... aren't welcome."

"But that's impossible. Discrimination on the basis of species is illegal!"

Goldfur's voice took on a harsh tone. "Sure it is, and you can see that there's no actual signs banning us. However, if you choose to go in there, you'll find that the service is terrible, the

food nearly inedible, and you'll probably be overcharged. There's not a lot that you can do about that."

I was shocked. From the news, I knew that there were some people who had a beef against morphs, but I'd never personally encountered it. I'd grown up in a mixed species neighbourhood, and while there were the typical childish pranks and cruelties, none of it had been specifically racially based. Then I'd gone into a career where humans were usually outnumbered by the various morph species, and there had never been this sort of trouble. My mind refused to cope with the illogical bias.

Lupu tugged on my arm. "C'mon, love, there are plenty of other good places to choose from." I let her pull me into motion, but that innocent green circle was now burned into my mind.

We ended up dining at a small family restaurant run by a dingo couple. The recent changes in attitude towards non-humans didn't seem to have affected their business much. Judging by the quality of the food that they served, I reckoned that it would take a lot more than a few disgruntled humans to change the opinions of their clientele, and I said as much. My complacency was shaken again when the male told me of a smear campaign accusing the restaurant of serving cat meat to humans, obviously playing on the fact that dingos were a breed of dog. It was a blatant fabrication, but much worse things had been done in human history and I was no longer prepared to jump to conclusions about the long-term success of their business. The thought that chilled me was that now I was a potential target too. The others didn't let me dwell on that though and they kept me well-entertained and fed. I enjoyed myself thoroughly, and I lost my self-consciousness completely. The dingo lady even complimented me on my top, and asked if I was a relative of Goldfur. I replied, "Something like that," with a smile.

After a long after-dinner conversation, we paid the bill and thanked our hosts before starting the walk back. We were passing a park when Lupu stopped and said to me, "Let's take a walk down by the lake!"

"Sure, if the others want to," I replied.

"No, silly!" she said, rolling her eyes. "I meant just us two."

"Oh!" I said brightly. "Well, yeah, I'd like that. Is it okay at this time of night?"

"Okay? It's perfect!"

I was a little puzzled by that reply, but otherwise I was unconcerned.

Lupu said to the others, "Me 'n Dale are goin' for a little stroll by ourselves. Seeya back home!"

The others smiled and waved us goodbye. A couple had big grins on their faces and I already had an inkling of what Lupu was up to. I'm not *that* naïve! In no great hurry, we walked arm in arm towards the calm waters where the moonlight reflected with hardly a ripple. Lupu was taking me into a textbook romantic scene, and I quite liked the idea. Without a word, we paused to admire the view, then she nudged me in the direction of the path around the lake's edge. After that evening's delicious meal and delightful conversation, this was the perfect way to end the day. The past few weeks of trials were pushed to the back of my mind and life seemed pretty damn good.

As we passed a clump of trees and bushes, Lupu paused. "Just a mo', love," she said as she disengaged her arm. She stepped forward and I saw that her ears were tilted alertly towards the bushes, and she was sniffing too. She turned back to me and said, "Come over here, Dale," before she disappeared through a slight gap in the shrubbery. Curiously I followed her only to be grabbed in a strong hug as Lupu started smothering me with wolfy kisses. Startled, it took me a moment to react, but then I started responding eagerly. After a bit of time, Lupu paused and smiled at me. "Welcome to Lovers' Grotto!"

I returned the smile. "Thanks! So you were trying to detect if anyone else was here first before inviting me in?"

"You got it. We're lucky tonight. This place is the worst kept secret in town and it's frequently in use."

"Oh well, if it had been, we still could have kissed elsewhere, you know?"

"Who said anything about just kissing?" she replied with a mischievous grin. She then put her hands on my jacket and started slipping it off.

"Wait! What do you think you're doing?" I asked, suddenly nervous again.

"Dale, dear, I said this was *Lovers'* Grotto, not Kissing Korner! This is where many of the local couples go for a naughty time under the stars."

"What...? You mean...?" I started protesting before her hand came up to close my muzzle.

"Dale, hon, for once just shut up and go with the moment."

She looked at me with a gaze that combined earnestness and desire. I started paying attention to the emotions that she was broadcasting and my empathic senses had been picking up but I'd been ignoring. With a small growl, I gave in to the inevitable. I wasn't annoyed; she just released my own pent-up desires. The jacket was soon joined on the ground by my fancy top and Lupu's blouse and we melted into each other's arms. That night, we made glorious love with only the heavens as our witness.

* * *

Six weeks ago I would have been quite shocked if somebody had suggested that I would find this new life becoming nearly routine. In fact, the day's activities had almost become predictable. Then I received a visit from the Star Corps scientists who headed up the team examining my problem.

After all the time waiting for news and never hearing anything, suddenly I was filled with trepidation. I realised that the semblance of normality that I had been experiencing was probably going to be upset again. My two visitors were Dr Kirrawong plus an ocelot morph whom I hadn't met yet, but turned out to be transporter specialist. He introduced himself as Martin Oss. No prizes for guessing where *that* surname came from! I asked Lupu and Forestwalker to join me, and I would have asked Goldfur too if shi hadn't been away at that time. They came straight to the point.

Kirrawong said, "I'm sorry, Dale, but we've come to the conclusion that giving you back your old body is an impossibility."

Oss added, "My team and I investigated every possibility, even some ridiculous ones, but the data we need to recreate your human form is just no longer there. The destruction of the transporter memory core was near complete and we were unable to retrieve any useable information. We can fully recreate the circumstances which gave you your new form, but without that data, we can't reproduce your original form."

Kirrawong took up the explanation. "However, we can offer you the next best thing. We can design a new human body for you using your parents' DNA as a starting point. We can select specific genes and combine them in such a way that the resulting form will have a similar height, build and distinguishing characteristics to what you used to have."

"Similar, but not the same?" I said.

"Correct. There's no complete record of your genetic structure, not to mention factors influenced by your environment as you grew up, so we would only making an educated guess.

However, you would be a normal, healthy male and a true genetic child of your parents."

"I see. Yet despite this, I would have to get used to another unfamiliar body, wouldn't I?"

"I'm afraid that you're right. No two humans, or any other species for that matter, learn how their body behaves in the same way. You will have to undergo physical therapy once again, just as you did to familiarise yourself with your chakat body."

I nodded, understanding the situation, but not keen on the thought of going through all that again. Another thought crossed my mind. "What about safety? My transformation was a million to one shot that I was lucky to survive. What risks are there with this procedure?"

Oss replied, "While there's no such thing as a perfectly safe procedure, we've been extensively testing it and have had no troubles at all. In fact, we had this pretty much worked out nearly a fortnight ago, but we spent this much time trying to make sure that we covered every possible contingency. We called in a specialist in genetic engineering, Professor Chakat Oceanwalker of Chakona, especially to help us with this. While shi wishes to pursue more research into transformations, shi's already quite satisfied with the reliability of the process. Combined with my knowledge of Transporter devices, I'm quite confident that the risk to you is negligible."

I mulled this over in my mind. I couldn't fault his explanation, but I still couldn't help feeling uneasy about going through that radical process once again without even the possibility of ever becoming my true self. "How long before I have to decide?" I asked them.

"There's no time limit on this, Mr Perkins," Oss replied. "Star Corps will allow you as much time as it takes to make your decision. However, we will need some warning to gather the necessary genetic samples from your parents and design your new body, so there won't be an instant response if you do make this choice."

"I understand." Then I surprised myself by saying, "Leave this with me for a while. I'll have to think it over." Up until this morning, I would have sworn that I would jump at the chance of getting a human body back again. The difficulty of getting used to that body was a factor in my hesitation, but certainly not the only one. I looked around me and saw Lupu's face. I'd invited her and the others to be with me while Kirrawong and Oss discussed my situation with me because I thought of them almost like my family now, and I felt that they should know what was happening. Besides, I wanted a bit of emotional support. Now I realised that there was more to it than that. Lupu was radiating a mixture of concern and hope, tinged with her own personal desires. The chakats who were aware of the empathic impressions were all projecting supportiveness with a touch of concern about the procedure. I think it was this moment when I realised that I had become as much a part of their lives as they had become part of mine. They truly cared, and this amazing Talent revealed it to me unfettered by misinterpretation or deceit. I knew that a large part of me wanted this to continue, and Lupu was the major factor.

I knew now that I was truly in love with Lupu. She had stolen my heart the first time we met, but I had come to appreciate her in many other ways since then. But how would she feel about having a human as a lover? And would the bond we shared be broken in the transformation? I found both possibilities dismaying. However, if I stayed, how would that affect her relationship with Goldfur and the rest of the family? She was hir denmate, and had a child between them to consider. Was I being selfish in wanting to replace Goldfur? I was torn, but this time I knew that I could talk with them and be guided truly. I owed it to them and Lupu. Turning back to the visitors, and getting up onto all fours, I said, "Thank you for the offer. I'll call you soon to let you know my decision."

Oss and Kirrawong got up from the sofa, recognising that this meeting was over. They said their farewells and I let them out them out the front door. Lupu had quietly padded up behind me, waiting for me to be done. She took my hand and brought me back to the others who were patiently waiting. Silently I settled back down on the lounging rug and waited for them to break the silence.

Goldfur was the first to speak. "Dale, we all want you to know that you're welcome to stay with us as long as you wish. Frankly, we like you a lot and would be quite happy for you to remain here with us." Shi gave me a lopsided grin. "Besides, we'd have to find another cubsitter!"

I smiled back at hir. I had been glad to do that chore. Frankly, I still felt as if I owed them all more than I could repay. "Thanks, Goldfur. I don't know if my destiny lies here, but I have to say it's one of the more pleasant alternatives."

"And what about us, hon?" Lupu asked.

Us. Not just her. I paused for a moment trying to choose my words. "Lupu, would you really feel the same about me if I became human again?"

"Dale, I love *you*, not just your physical form. I decided a fair while ago that I wanted to be with you no matter what."

I felt a little ashamed. She had given me her love unreservedly, and here I was still dithering. I made up my mind about one thing right there. I took her hands and looked her in the eyes. "Lupu, will you be my mate?" I simply asked.

She threw her arms about me in a fierce hug. "Of course I will!" she exclaimed as she lick-kissed me madly.

I laughed and tried to give as good as I got. It was a while before I became aware of the cheers, claps and congratulations coming from the others, but I put one arm about Lupu and faced them to acknowledge and thank them all. When that was done, I said, "I feel much better now, but I still have to make my decision.

Anyone got any last moment thoughts or suggestions."

Forestwalker spoke up. "Dale, we think you'd be a fine person no matter what form you decide to take, but I have to say that I think that you'll make a good chakat. Look how far you've come in six weeks."

Shi was right. Nobody had questioned my nature in all the outings since the celebration dinner. Given a bit more education and time to get used to some of the more unusual customs, I reckon that I could pass as a chakat for the rest of my life. "Still, I've got a lifetime of experience as a human, and I know that you'd still be my friends, and mate…" I added, glancing lovingly at Lupu, "…if I choose to take their offer."

Lupu said, "Hon, there's one other thing that I feel you should know before you make that decision, and now that you've asked me to be your mate, perhaps you'll see that I'm not using it as a bargaining tool."

When she hesitated, I said curiously, "Well? Spit it out!"

"I'm pregnant. Just to be sure there's no misunderstanding, yes, you're the father."

The news left me stunned. "But… *when*…?" I stammered.

"Back at Lover's Grotto," she replied.

"But… you weren't in heat then, were you? I would have smelled it!"

"Dale, love, believe it or not, we females don't always want to smell like a bitch in heat. There are fragrances that can mask the scent, and I was using one for our night out."

"Did you plan to get pregnant?"

"No hon, I honestly only used the fragrance purely for

perfume purposes that night. I admit though that my horniness was a strong factor in asking you to go with me into the park though. I suppose if I stopped and thought about it, I would have realised what I was risking, but frankly I didn't care to think of the alternative, so I blocked it from my mind. Later when I realised that I had conceived, I didn't tell you because I thought you might think I was using it as a bargaining tool, and I wanted you to ask me to be your mate without that hanging over your head. Now however, I think you need to consider the child when you make your decision."

She was right. I *would* have thought that she had ulterior motives. As much as I'd acquired chakat traits, I was still a human at the core. That shook me a little. I didn't *want* those feelings. I was spoiled by the clean honesty of these people. Could I aspire to that honesty and still take back human form? Maybe, but it would be hard; perhaps too hard for me. I finally replied to Lupu. "You're right, I do. Will you take a walk with me, hon?" I offered her my arm.

"Gladly!" she replied, slipping her arm around mine.

We left the others and walked outside. Leisurely and aimlessly, we meandered in the general direction of the forest. We took one of the paths that were used for hiking and I drank in the sights, sounds and especially the scents with a new appreciation. I would give up so much of that if I became a man again. And there was the feel of my powerful form effortlessly negotiating the terrain and the pleasant feel of the breeze in my fur. If you had to trade bodies, a chakat's was by far a very good choice. I admired Lupu – lean, strong and a beauty in her own right. Not sleek like a chakat, but rugged and wild in a way that always excited me. She caught me looking at her and smiled, but didn't interrupt my thoughts. Then there was the child now growing in her belly. I had wanted one since considering asking Mary-Anne to marry me, although now I knew that I was a little starry-eyed at the time. Having experienced the family's cubs though, I knew much of what was involved, and I suddenly realised that I wanted this child very much. I caressed Lupu's side. She lifted an eyebrow and gave me a knowing grin. She wanted this cub as much as I did! Then there was feeding hir.

I stopped walking. Lupu looked at me quizzically. I said, "You couldn't have this cub and stay in the pack, could you? I'm told that the child of a chakat and another taur is always a chakat, correct?" She nodded, waiting to see where I was going with this. "But a chakat cub *has* to have chakat milk to grow healthily and if I choose to become a human again, you'd have to return here when shi's born. Right?"

"That's right. I didn't bring this up because I didn't want to influence your decision unduly…"

I interrupted her. "Don't you think I might *want* to have a say in the upbringing of our child? Hell! Just moments ago I was daydreaming about what it would be like to breastfeed my own flesh and blood!"

Lupu could have gotten annoyed at my attitude, but instead she latched onto what I had just said. "*Our* child? Your flesh and blood? Shi wouldn't be if you became human."

"I know, and I want hir to be able to have a sire that shi can relate to. I want to be able to play with hir without worrying whether shi'd harm me accidentally with hir greater strength and mass. I want hir to hear me purr my pleasure when shi makes me happy."

"Sounds to me like you're trying to find reasons to stay a chakat," shi observed.

"Yeah. I gotta have some reasons to give to my parents when I inform them of my decision. If I return to human form, they'll expect me to justify myself in regards to caring for our cub. If I stay a chakat, then their son is forever changed. This decision is getting more complicated all the time!"

"Dale, however good your parents are, you owe it to

yourself to put your own needs first. Then think of mine. As your mate, I think I deserve at least second place?"

"Yes you do! You're probably right about the rest too." I paused, thinking furiously and getting nowhere. Then I looked at Lupu again, an aura of hopefulness about her. My thoughts slid off on a tangent. "Lupu love, would you consummate our mating with me right here and now?"

I had managed to startle her. Flustered, she took a moment to get her thoughts together before replying. "Sure!" She looked around and indicated a slightly open area with a bit of grass. "How about there? It looks okay, although we'll need a grooming later."

I took her hand and gently pulled her in that direction. "I don't care about that. I want to make love with you, and I want it to be my choice. This may be the last chance I'll have before committing myself one way or the other, and I want to legitimise our child."

She looked very happy, but even then she argued me. "Legitimacy is such a human concept!"

"That's who you'll be mating with, dear. Take it or leave it!"

"I'll take it! I'll take it!" she laughed and pulled me down onto the grass to start smothering me in wolfy kisses.

I enjoyed the kisses and gave as good as I got. We spent a lot of time enjoying touching and petting before I decided to bring things to conclusion. I put my hands on either side of her face and looked deep into her eyes. "Lupu, will you be my denmate and share my life? Will you help me bring up our child as happily as those of Goldfur and Forest?"

"Of course I will! But that isn't the proper chakat ritual!" she protested.

"I'm not a proper chakat," I reminded her. "In return, I promise to do the same." Then I kissed her long and deep. Before long, I moved to mount her, and we made passionate love as mates for the first time.

* * *

"They're back!" Forest called out to the others as we returned to the house.

Within moments, all the chakats and Trina had converged on us, soon followed by a more laid-back Garrek. If Kris had been there, I suspect he would have been with Garrek, chuckling over the fuss the others were making. There was no point in playing innocent. They'd guessed that I'd been thinking over my choice and wouldn't be returning without having made a decision. I asked them all to gather in the living room. I kept an arm about Lupu who was saying nothing. She just kept her head against my shoulder with a look of contentment on her face. I felt much the same way, but I knew I wouldn't be allowed to escape that easily. When everyone was ready, I began the little speech I'd been rehearsing in my mind.

"Firstly, let me thank you all for helping and guiding me through all this. My life has certainly become more interesting since the accident, but I think it's mostly been for the good. Bearing all this in mind and the talk I just had with Lupu, I've made my decision... I'm going to remain a chakat!"

"Yay! Told ya!" Forest said to Goldfur.

"So who was disagreeing?" shi retorted.

I grinned, then continued. "Allow me to introduce myself. I am Chakat Goldendale, child of Rose and Edward, but please keep calling me Dale for short if you wish. I'm very pleased to be part of your family."

There were cheers and clapping. I was also given the more

traditional chakat hugs, and this time I enjoyed and returned them all enthusiastically.

"Great choice of name!" Midnight said.

"You're going to love being a chakat," Forestwalker predicted.

"You've stolen a good mate!" Goldfur had a light-hearted dig at me.

"Just wait until you have that child. Then you'll *really* know what it's like to look after kits!" Garrek predicted.

"Wanna threesome?" Trina asked before running away shrieking in laughter as both Lupu and I threw lounge cushions at her.

Even Eudora had a say: "Auntie Dale!!"

We all laughed and I gave hir a hug too.

I stood up and looked around me. Never in my life had I such a big family. Sure, it was mostly a family of friends, but they were the best people one could wish for, and I would be counting on them for more instruction for the immediate future. My decision made, I felt a load lift from my shoulders, leaving a sense of purpose in its place. There was just one more thing left to be said.

"From now on," I started loudly to make sure I had everyone's attention, "I wish to be treated entirely as a chakat. One who needs a little help perhaps, but no longer a hapless human. You can stop saying '*he*' and '*him*' in regards to me because I accept that I will be a herm from now on. After all, I *am* a chakat!

ILLUSTRATIONS

Page 6: *My Twin Sisters* by Roy D. Pounds II
Page 10: *Commander Redfang* by James L. Brandt
Page 12: *Stumbling* by Julie Wondra
Page 14: *My... Tail?* by Bernard Doove
Page 16: *Space Chakat* by Terry Knight
Page 28: *Trina's Study* by Steve Gallacci
Page 30: *I'm In The Mood* by Roy D. Pounds II
Page 41: *BBV – Big Breasted Vixen* by Bernard Doove
Page 43: *Dale and Mary-Anne* by Heather Bruton
Page 46: *Lupu* by Mayra Boyle
Page 55: *Checking Hirself Over* by Stephie Stone
Page 60: *I Can't Eat All That!* by Roy D. Pounds II
Page 91: *Training* by Kacey Miyagami
Page 102: *Distressed* by Kacey Miyagami
Page 120: *Souvenirs* by Kacey Miyagami
Page 133: *Get It Off!* by Roy D. Pounds II
Page 135: *Windrunner's Birth* by Roy D. Pounds II
Page 138: *Trina* by SketchMuffin
Page 143: *Furries Not Welcome* by Roy D. Pounds II
Page 145: *Dining Out* by Kacey Miyagami
Page 147: *Park Stroll* by Megan Giles
Page 153: *Lupu Excited* by Opal Weasel
Page 158: *Prelude To Mating* by Xian Jaguar

Made in the USA
Charleston, SC
14 August 2013